TETHERED TO HIM

KYLIE KENT

If you want early access to everything, yes everything come and join my Patreon Group
Kylie Kent Patreon

Want to be involved in discussions and have access to tons of give-aways? Join my readers group on Facebook Kylie's Steam Room

Social Media:

Website & Newsletter: www.kyliekent.com
Facebook: @kyliekent2020
Instagram Follow: @author_kylie_kent_

kylie kent
SEXY, ALWAYS AND FOREVER ROMANCE

Ebook ISBN 13: 978-1-922816-05-4
Paperback ISBN 13: 978-1-922816-19-1

Cover illustration by
RJ CREATIVES GRAPHIC SERVICES

Editing services provided by
Kat Pagan – https://www.facebook.com/PaganProofreading

To my amazing team of people that tirelessly have supported me throughout this authoring journey. Amy, Mel, Natasha, Sam & Vicki , I could not do this without you.

PROLOGUE

Two pink lines. I'm staring at the stick that's just changed my life forever. I've always loved the colour pink. It was my favourite, but right now, on this stick, I could use a little less of the ominous hue. My hands tremble. Pregnant. What the hell am I going to do? I'm eighteen years old. I've only just finished high school. I can't be pregnant.

Except, according to this stick and the ten others

still lined up on the bench, I very much am. Shit. I can't do this. How can I do this? The one person I want to call, the one person who should be helping me figure this out... can't. He can't help me because he left. I hate him. He left and now I have to figure all of this out myself.

"Ava, hurry up. I need a lift to the gym." My little brother bangs on my bedroom door. When I say little, I mean younger, because there is nothing little about Axel at sixteen. He's already six foot tall, and on a mission to bulk up to be the next Hulk. Hence why he's spending all of his time at my aunt and uncle's gym.

"Yeah, hang on a minute," I yell back, attempting to keep the violent shake my whole body is experiencing out of my voice. Picking up the bundle of tests, I take them into my closet and shove them in a shoe box, before pushing everything towards the back, burying it with a pile of other shoe boxes. I don't really need to hide them. It's not like anyone will come in here. My parents are not the type to snoop. They trust me. I've never given them a reason not to.

I was a straight-A student. I just graduated high school at the top of my class. I spend all of my spare time studying and dancing. My whole life revolves around one objective. To dance on stage for The Australian Ballet Company as a prima ballerina. I'm currently a lead dancer with The Sydney Ballet. My dream audition is in four weeks' time. I've postponed university for twelve months. And I've put all of my cookies in this one life goal: getting this position. Those two pink lines have just taken *that* dream and blew it to high hell. I'm never going to get to dance professionally now.

I hate him. Bloody Noah. He should be here to help me through this. This isn't just my stuff up; it's his too. I hate him for leaving me. I hate that, even when I say it out loud, I can hear the lie in my own voice. As much as I want to hate him, I can't. And I hate that even more.

1

Six months earlier

I really, really should have stayed home. Why did I let Sophia talk me into coming to this party? It's full of underage drunken teens. Boys, whose hands like to land on places they weren't invited. And girls, who want to use me in hopes they can get closer to my brothers.

Yes, *brothers*. Plural. The girls in my year go nuts over Ash, even though he's ten years older than me. He'd never touch any of them. But they won't go down without trying to gain his attention. Then there's Axel. He's two years younger, but that doesn't stop the girls from vying for his attention. He laps it up too, uses it to his whoreish advantage. Meaning I never truly know if these girls like me for me, or if they like me on the off-chance they might get close to one of my siblings.

"Sophia, seriously, why are we here?"

"Because you only turn eighteen once, baby, and we need to celebrate." She's been using my birthday as an excuse to party for days now. It's not my birthday for another two weeks.

"Again, it's not my birthday yet," I yell back at her over the music.

"Two more weeks of being a juvenile, Ava. We need to get up to as much mischief while we still can. Here, bottoms up."

I take the pink bottle Sophia shoves into my chest. She's already had three of these—I've been counting. I'm the responsible one. The good one. The one who makes sure she doesn't do anything stupid. Like getting shit-faced on a Sunday night before exams.

"No, we're not drinking anymore. You need some water. Come on." I drag her into the kitchen and hunt down the fridge to find some water. Finally locating a bottle shoved up the back I retrieve it and hand it to her.

"Fine, but we're not leaving yet. I told Jasper I'd meet him here."

At that, I roll my eyes. Of course she did. Jasper is Sophia's on-again-off-again boyfriend of three years. They must be *on* right now. I really can't keep up anymore. Twisting our hands together, we make our way through the crowd, or more like I let Sophia drag me behind her.

We find Jasper outside, sitting around with his mates. They all whistle as they see us approach. I cringe at the thought of having to fight off these assholes all night. I really can't handle their attempts at flirting for the next few hours.

"Are you planning on getting a ride home with Jasper?" I ask Sophia, praying that she says yes and I don't have to stick around any longer.

"Yes, but please don't leave, Ava." She pouts out her bottom lip.

"Cute. But I really want to go home. I'm sorry... I'll make it up to you. I heard Ash is going away next weekend. We'll have a little get-together at his place."

My friends love hanging out in the penthouse. Ash hasn't figured out that I use his place for my slumber parties, so as long as I can get away with it, I will. Truthfully, I think he actually knows but chooses not to say anything. Either way, I'll use it to my benefit.

"Argh, fine. Do you want me to come with you? Just let me say goodbye to Jasper."

"No, stay. I'm fine. I'm just going to go home and

crash anyway." I'm not lying. I'm dead tired. It was a gruelling rehearsal this afternoon at the dance academy. But I'm about to be picked up by Australia's top dance company. I can't *not* be in top shape.

"Okay, love ya. Drive safe and text me when you get home."

"Back at ya, babe." I wave with a relieved smile as I exit the door.

However, both that smile and relief instantly wash away when I get to my car and see the front tires slashed. Who would slash one of my tires? I pull out my phone. Shit... Who do I call? If I call my dad, he's going to be pissed I was even at a party on a Sunday. Ash... I'm going to have to call Ash.

"Hey, baby, need a hand there?"

Chills—and not the good kind—run through my body. I'm a few houses down from where the party is raging on, and there's no one out here. It's dark. Well, I guess there's someone out here; he's just someone I wish wasn't.

"No, my brother's on his way. Thanks though." I unlock my car, fully intending to sit inside with the doors locked until I can contact Ash. However, just as I open the door, Trevor reaches out and slams it shut. Pinning my body between the car and his much larger frame, he runs his fingers down the length of my arm. My eyes dart around as far as I can see, looking for something. Anything. "Trevor, move. Get off me." My voice is calm, much calmer than the panic currently wreaking havoc inside my head.

"Now why would I do that, baby. I know you want me. I've seen the way you look at me. You and me, we're going to be so good together."

What the hell is he on?

"No." I bring my knee up, connecting it with his balls.

I guess I didn't hit hard enough because he doesn't tumble over like I thought he would. Instead, he raises an arm and backhands me across the face. Before I can figure out what's going on, I feel the weight of his body being pulled off me. It takes a minute for my brain to register what's happening. To see that Trevor is now on the ground with a huge guy on top of him, slamming punch after punch into his face.

Shit, he needs to stop before he kills him. I mean, I wanted him off and away from me, but I didn't want him dead.

"Stop, you're going to kill him." I reach out and grab the stranger's shoulder. And the moment my hand connects with his skin, I get shocked with a thousand lightning bolts running right up my arm. I quickly pull back.

What the hell was that?

The guy stops, glances my way, and curses under his breath. I watch, unable to do anything else as he stands to his full height. I have to crane my neck to look up at him. I couldn't get the slimeball Trevor off me, so I have no chance at defending myself against this guy.

I know he's two years older than me. He went to my school. Noah Hunt. I know of him, but I don't *know* him.

"Are you okay?" His deep husky voice sends chills down my spine.

"Ah, yeah. Thank you." I peek down at Trevor, who is stumbling to his feet before he looks at Noah, then turns and walks away.

"Come on, I'll take you home," Noah says, like it's a foregone conclusion. Like I'm expected to just jump in the car with him.

"I'm fine. I'm going to call my brother to get me." I pull out my phone for a second time.

Noah tilts his head as he looks me up and down. I'm wearing a blue sundress that falls just short of my knees and a pair of white Louboutin sandals. The warm night air suddenly has a chill to it, or maybe it's just the way Noah's eyes devour me. When his gaze settles on my face, the interest I saw in them turns into what appears to be rage. He takes one step forward and grabs my chin between his fingers, angling my face to the side.

"He fucking hit you?" he snarls.

I'm not sure if that was a question or a statement, so I don't answer it. "It's okay. I'll be fine."

"I should go back and finish him off," he says under his breath.

"What?"

"Nothing. Come on, I'm taking you home." When I don't budge, he smirks. "Ava, if I wanted to hurt you, I wouldn't be standing here talking to you, babe. I'm not the bad guy here. But if you insist on calling your brother, go ahead. I'll wait with you until he gets here."

"You don't need to do that."

"Yes, I do."

I quickly dial Ash. The phone rings out. "Damn it, Ash," I huff. He always picks up when I call. Then I remember he was going to Brisbane last week. Is he even back yet? "I can call Chase. He'll come get me," I say out loud, knowing my brother's best friend will jump to my rescue.

Noah emits what sounds like a growl. "Babe, we can stand here all night going through your contact list, or you can just accept a ride from a friend who's already here."

"Friend? I don't know you." I laugh.

"Yes, you do. We went to school together."

"You were two grades above me. I don't know you, Noah," I tell him again.

"See? You know my name. You know my graduating year. Like I said, we're old friends."

"Okay, but if you try any funny business, know that I know people who know people," I warn him.

"Well, I would hate to have to face the people who know the people you know." He lifts an eyebrow, and I can't help but laugh. "Come on, my car's just up the road." He takes my palm in his, intertwining our fingers together as we walk in that direction. I look down at our joined hands. His is so large and warm. An odd feeling of safety wraps around me.

He stops at a black Lamborghini Huracán. There *is* one thing I know about Noah Hunt and that is the fact that his family is loaded. Old money. He was also the 'it' kid in school. He'd have girls fawning all over him at every opportunity. I don't remember him ever reciprocating though. Maybe he's gay?

"Are you gay?" I blurt out. *Yep, way to play it cool in front of the hot guy, Ava.*

"What? Definitely not gay," he says, running his eyes up and down my body again before opening the door. "Get in."

I sink down into the luxurious seats. It's not the first time I've been in a vehicle like this. My dad and my brother have a penchant for fancy cars that cost enough to feed a whole third-world country.

"So, what about my car makes you think I'm gay?" Noah asks as he starts the engine.

"It's not the car. I was just remembering the times I saw you at school. You never had a girlfriend—well, not that I knew of anyway."

"That's because the girl I wanted barely knew I existed."

The snort that escapes me comes out on its own accord. "Please, every girl at school practically threw themselves at you."

"You didn't," he counters, looking at me.

Shit, what do I say to that? I've never been interested in having a boyfriend. I've always been too focused on my goal. There's no room for anything else. That's not to say I don't notice and appreciate a good-looking guy. "I don't fawn over guys. I have plans, and those plans don't include boys." I shrug.

2

Noah

She's in my car. I have fucking Ava Williamson in my car.

For three years, I've watched this girl from the side lines. Silently observing her shine in everything that she does. I've admired her determination, her grit and strength. I've been to her shows, sat in the back, and been in total awe over how graceful she is up on that stage.

She just asked me why I didn't have a girlfriend in high school. I did, before I first laid eyes on her in that drama room. I was in my senior year, ready to graduate, sign up to the defence, and get out of this town.

Then I saw her. Everything changed that day. What I thought I wanted out of life went out the window. And all I could think about was Ava. Her vision haunted my every waking hour, and she was there again when I would close my eyes at night.

I kept my distance, because a girl like Ava Williamson did not belong with a guy like me. I wasn't bad, *per se*. I just knew I wasn't good either. I knew I would only taint and ruin something as pure and perfect as the girl beside me. I shouldn't be anywhere near her, and suddenly I find myself in my car. With her. Driving slower than necessary because I'm not ready to let her out. "I want to take you somewhere. Show you something." I turn the corner and make a detour.

"Where?" she asks.

"It's somewhere I go when I need to think. A place I want to share with you." I play it off like it isn't anything special.

In reality, it's the very spot I've imagined proposing to this girl; it's the location I've envisioned marrying her. With all of her family and friends there watching. My side can read about it in the fucking announcements section of the *Sydney Herald* for all I care. If I ever woke up in a parallel universe where Ava was mine, I'd make sure my family never got a foot near her.

To say that they're toxic would be an understatement. If you look up *dysfunctional* in the dictionary, I'm sure you'd see a picture of my parents. On the outside, they look like the ideal power couple. United on all fronts. Supportive of each other's goals and achievements. On the inside, behind closed doors, my parents occupy separate wings of the house, unable to stand the very sight of each other.

If they were any other couple, I'm sure they would have divorced twenty years ago. But they're Hunts, and Hunts don't divorce. We don't shame the family name. We don't attract unwanted media attention. And we don't conduct ourselves in any way that would appear distasteful to the public eye.

Why?

It comes down to two things: money and power. It's that simple. The Hunt name is associated with wealth. And with wealth, comes the power to rule the Australian business scene.

I'm my parents' biggest disappointment. Their only child, not wanting to take over the family business. I did sign up for the Army, joined right out of high school. I don't regret it for one minute. It got me out of there and away from here. For the last year, I've been living up in North Queensland. Far away from the temptation that I have strapped into the seat next to me.

"Where is this place? I have early rehearsals," Ava says.

"It's not much farther," I lie. It's not like she can escape now.

"Okay."

"What are your plans after graduation?" I ask, like I don't already know.

"I'm going to dance for The Australian Ballet," she says it like it's a fact. Like there's no other possibility for her future.

"Really? That's impressive. Did you audition yet?"

"My audition isn't until February, but I'm preparing for it now. I'll be ready."

"You dance for another company, right? For The Sydney Ballet?" Again, I already know this. My mother made me attend a show a few months back when I was in town. To my surprise, the show was anything but boring, and it had everything to do with Ava being the one up on that stage.

I could watch her dance for hours and not get tired of seeing how her body twists and turns so delicately. There are other things I want to see her body do as I bend her in ways I imagine a ballerina of her calibre would be able to manage.

Shifting in my seat, I adjust my pants, making room for my growing fucking cock. I need a distraction. I need something else to talk about. Anything. "Do you have pets?"

"No, do you?"

"Nope."

"What have you been doing the last few years?" she asks. Thank fuck at least one of us has some conversational skills.

"I joined the Army, got posted up in Townsville."

"That seems dangerous. Why would you do that?"

At her scolding tone, I glance over and see her face scrunched up as she gives me a weird look. Is she worried? Disgusted? I can't fucking tell. "It's no more dangerous than any other job."

"Other jobs don't have you going to war. I'd say it's way more dangerous."

"I'm careful, babe. You don't have to worry about me."

"I'm not worried. Why would I be worried? I don't even know you."

"Sure." I smile at her. *She's worried.* My heart does a little fucking flip with the realization. "Why were you at that party tonight? You don't seem like the type of girl who parties."

"Really? What type of girl do I seem like?"

"The good type."

"Right, because I am. I have to be if I want to make my dream come true."

"Good girls can still have fun, you know."

"Dancing is fun," she replies quickly.

"So what were you doing at the party?" I repeat the unanswered question.

"Sophia, my friend, wanted to go. She has it in her head that we need to celebrate my birthday every day for the next two weeks."

"You're turning eighteen, right?"

"Yep. Can't wait."

Me fucking too. I know at seventeen she's far from jailbait, but fuck, it still seems fucking wrong to have the thoughts I have about her in my head. At least when she's eighteen, it won't be as bad. Hopefully.

We drive in what I assume is a comfortable silence. Judging by the way Ava relaxes back into the headrest, her shoes kicked off and her bare feet resting on the edge of the seat, I'd say she's comfortable. I wouldn't normally let anyone put their feet on my interior like that. But when it comes to Ava, I can't seem to tell her otherwise.

An hour and a half later, I pull into the empty carpark. It's always empty up here at night. It's why I like to visit; it's an escape from the noise and bustle of the city. "We're here."

Ava pokes her head around the windows as she scopes out our location. "Where exactly is here?" she asks.

"It's a little lookout I stumbled across a while ago." We're up in the Blue Mountains. It's the most beautiful scenic area close to Sydney.

I jump out of the car and jog around to her side. She already has the door open before I get the chance to do it for her. After she's slipped her feet back into her shoes, she steps out and spins around in a circle. "There's no one here," she observes.

"That's not true. We're here." I take her hand and lead her over to the large lookout platform. At this time of night, you can't see much. It's pitch black, which is why I love it. You can imagine you're looking out onto anything.

"Um, Noah, it's dark. There's nothing to see."

"There's plenty to see. Come on, sit down with me." I lower myself to the ground and wait for her to sit beside me. She brings her knees up to her chest and rests her head on them, looking at me with those ocean-blue eyes of hers. "What do you see when you look out there?" I ask her, pointing to the darkness.

"I don't see anything," she says again.

"Wrong. You're just not looking properly. This is the very place where you can see whatever you want to see. You have dreams of seeing yourself on the stage for The Australian Ballet? Look out into the darkness and see that," I tell her.

She turns her head and peers out into the nothingness, quietly observing whatever it is she's envisioning. A lone tear slips down her cheek. Fuck.

I bring my thumb up and wipe it away. "What's wrong? What did you see?"

"I saw it. I saw myself dancing on stage. What if..." She leaves her unspoken question hanging between us.

"What if *what*?"

"What if this is the only way I'll ever see it? What if I don't make it? I planned my whole life around this one dream. What if I can't do it?"

"You are Ava fucking Williamson. You can do anything you put your mind to, babe. You're amazingly talented—seeing you dance is one of the best memories I have. It would be a shame if the whole world doesn't get to witness that," I tell her a little too much.

"You've seen me dance?"

"A few times. My mother is a fan of the ballet," I lie. My mother is a fan of *being seen* at events.

"Oh." She looks back out into the darkness. "What do you see when you come here?"

"Peace," I mumble the singular word. She shivers as she wraps her arms around herself. Tugging my Henley over my head, I pass it to her. "Put this on. You're cold."

Her mouth is open wide in shock. "I'm not taking your shirt off you, Noah. Then you'll be cold," she argues while her eyes travel up and down my chest and abs.

I smirk. "Yeah, I think I'll be okay, babe. Besides, I've got another one in the car if I need it." I pull the shirt over her head, and she shoves her arms through the sleeves.

"Thank you."

"I should get you home. Are you going to be okay? Will your folks be wondering where you are?"

"They think I'm sleeping at Sophia's tonight," she says. "But it's fine. I can get in without waking them."

"Okay. Let's go." I push to my feet and hold out my hand to her. When she places her palm in mine, I swear I feel an electric current run up my arm.

She must feel it too, as she quickly attempts to pull back. But I hold on tight, tugging her to an upright position. I don't let go of her hand as I lead her to the car. She's silent as she slips back inside. Just as I'm pulling out of the carpark, she turns to face me. "Noah, will you bring me here again?".

"Anytime, babe. All ya gotta do is ask, and I'll take you anywhere you want to go."

She offers a shy smile before she looks out the window. I mean it. I have the ability to take her anywhere. I know she's seen the world; she's well-travelled. And her family is hardly on the poverty line. She's wearing fifteen-hundred-dollar shoes for fuck's sake. The Williamsons just aren't the Hunt kind of wealthy.

An hour and a half later, I'm pulling up in front of her parents' place. I don't want to let her go; though I know I have to.

"Thank you for the lift, and for showing me the lookout spot." She peeks up at me with that smile again. Everything in me wants to reach over and kiss her. Pull her across the centre console and settle her on my lap. I don't though. Instead, I lean to the side and kiss her cheek.

"It was my pleasure, babe." Then I watch as she opens the gate, closes it behind her, and walks up the driveway. I don't turn my engine back on and pull away until I see her pass through the front door.

3

I wake up with a smile on my face when my alarm goes off at six in the morning. Did I dream that? Or did I really go to a deserted lookout point with Noah Hunt last night?

I get up and head for my adjoining bathroom, tripping over the shoes I left discarded on the floor. Judging by the dirt clinging to their heels, it wasn't a dream. I really was in Noah's car, and he really did kiss my cheek. I know it seems juvenile but *he kissed me.* Do I wish he would have just grabbed my face and slammed his lips to mine with passion and fire? Yes.

I've never been kissed like that. I've kissed a few boys a few times. I just didn't feel anything. I didn't like it. But with Noah? Just his lips on my cheek had me heating up. Imagine what it'd feel like if those lips were on mine?

I turn the water on scalding hot, hoping it will soothe my aching muscles. It won't. Nothing ever does. It's one of the pitfalls of being a dancer. Continuous sore muscles and blistered feet. I've learned to embrace it. If I'm not aching, I'm not dancing right, not trying hard enough. Sinking under the water, I pour soap onto my loofah.

Images of Noah flash in my mind. His smile. His eyes. I want to look at his eyes more. His body... When he took his shirt off, I almost combusted. I knew he worked out, but damn. I've spent plenty of time in the gym—my aunt and uncle own a chain of them. My uncle insisted on teaching me how to box, not that those lessons did me any good last night with Trevor.

What would have happened if Noah hadn't been there? The way he came to my defence... How he beat into Trevor... The violence... It should repulse me. *Scare me.* Yet it only drives my desire for him more. It's demented.

Not that it matters. Noah Hunt would never be

interested in a girl like me. *A good girl* is what he called me.

And it's what I am.

I rush through my shower, then throw on some clothes and makeup. I refuse to leave the house without a completely done-up face. It's my shield, my mask. I like to look good. I feel good when I look good. I need to get to my car, maybe try to call Ash again to see if he can get my tire fixed.

I manage to walk out the door without running into my family. Axe won't show his face until late in the afternoon. And my parents—well, I don't even want to know why they love sleeping in so late.

Pulling out my phone, I contemplate calling my older brother. It's early and he works late. He manages the family's chain of nightclubs. He loves it, and he's turned one nightclub into an empire all around the country.

I look up and have to do a double take. My car is sitting in my driveway. How the hell did that get there? I walk around to the passenger's side, where the tire was slashed, and see a brand-new one in its place.

Uh...

Opening the door, I find the keys in the ignition. My eyebrows immediately draw down. I don't remember leaving my keys with the car. As I go to place my handbag on the seat next to me, I see a note and pick it up.

Ava,

I've put a new spare in your boot. If you ever get stuck again, call me.

Or if you just want to escape for a little while, call me.

Noah

He jotted his number at the bottom of the page. Adding his name to my contact list, I then send him a message.

Me: Thank you for replacing my tire. Let me know how much I owe you and I'll fix you up.

The little dots appear on my screen almost immediately, and the message is marked as being read. I wait a few minutes expecting a reply. When one doesn't come, I make sure I entered the number correctly. And I did.

Throwing my phone down on the seat, I put the car into drive. I need to get to the studio. I don't have time to sit around and wait for some guy to respond to a message. I'm not that girl. Although, it appears I am *that girl.* Because the moment I stop in the studio's parking lot, the first thing I do is check to see if he's replied.

He hasn't. *Shocker.* I don't know why I'm surprised. He's Noah freaking Hunt. Way out of my league, not that I want him to be in my league. It would just be polite if he acknowledged my message.

I manage to put him out of my mind the moment my feet hit the stage. This is my happy place, where all thoughts empty from my head and I lose myself in the movements. By the time we've nearly perfected the routine, my whole body is aching, I'm dripping with sweat, and I'm starved.

I shower and change into my school uniform, then say my goodbyes to my dance partners. Again, I check my phone and find no message from Noah. There is, however, a string of texts from Sophia.

Sophia: Tiny dancer, hit me up when you're finished rehearsals. We need to celebrate.

Sophia: I have an idea. You're going to love it.

I'm almost too scared to ask, so I continue reading.

Sophia: Tiny dancer, meet me in the library at lunch.

I respond with a thumbs up and a love heart emoji.

THE WHOLE MORNING HAS SUCKED. I might have been able to get the thoughts of Noah out of my head while I was on stage, but the same can't be said for during class hours. I've made myself sick with reasons why he hasn't responded to my messages.

Reason number one: He's been put on a helicopter and is landing in the middle of a war zone as we speak.

Reason number two: He's been injured training at work. It can't be safe to play with guns and bombs all day, can it? Is that even what he does? I have no idea.

Reason number three: He just doesn't want to speak to me ever again.

Reason number four: He has a girlfriend I don't know about—*that one* actually has my hand wrapped around my phone a little tighter. If he had a girlfriend, why would he kiss me? Okay, I know *technically* it was completely PG. A little peck on the cheek. Nothing really. Except it made me feel something. Everything.

Reason number five: He was in a horrific car accident and is fighting for his life in surgery.

Reason number six: He was bitten by a snake and is slowly dying somewhere in the bush.

Reason number seven: He was bitten by a funnel web and is already dead.

I think you get the picture. There could be a million reasons why he hasn't messaged me back. None of which suggest a good outcome.

I have to forget about him. He's taken up way too much space in my mind this morning. I liked it better when I thought he didn't know my name. When, just a few years ago, I'd steal glances at him in the hallways at school.

I make my way to the library to see whatever trouble Sophia is cooking up now. When I get there, I head straight for our spot. It's a little tucked away study room we've been using since we were juniors. Pushing the door open, I'm stunned speechless.

"Surprise," Sophia whispers. "Come in. Shut the door."

My mouth salivates the second I enter the room. I eye the setup she has on the table. I don't even know how she's managed all this. Turning my attention to the other occupants, I see our friends Hannah and Kia. "How? What? How did you girls do this? It looks amazing."

Covering the table is an assortment of fruits, veggie sticks, cheeses, and cold meats. In the middle is an ice bucket with a bottle of champagne. I pick up a grape and pop it into my mouth. I'm not sure how they think we're getting away with drinking during school hours. Although, with the morning I've had, I wouldn't mind a glass or two to take my mind off a certain soldier. Surely I can make it through the last few hours of school a little tipsy. How hard can it be?

"Pour me a glass." I point to the bottle. All three girls glare at me in shock. I know... I'm the good girl. The girl who would never drink on a school night, let alone *at* school. "What? It's my birthday celebration, isn't it?" I answer their questioning looks.

"It is. Let's do this." Sophia pours four glasses, handing one to each of us. "A toast. To Ava, our very own tiny dancer. May all your steps be perfect and all your toes recover from the years of abuse. And if they don't, I'll take your shoe collection off your hands when you're stuck wearing Crocs." She shivers with disgust at the same time I scrunch up my nose.

"If I ever have to wear Crocs, just pull the plug, girls."

The rest of lunch is filled with laughter and jokes

about ugly shoes. I haven't thought about Noah's lack of messages much at all. That is, until I stop in the girls' bathroom on the way to class. A little lightheaded, I pop a Panadol and down almost a whole bottle of water. And before I can talk myself out of it, I hit dial on his number.

He answers pretty much straight away. "Ava, everything okay?"

"Is this Noah Hunt speaking?" I ask him.

"Pretty sure you rang me, babe. You don't know whose number you dialled?"

I can hear the laughter in his voice, which just pisses me off. "Oh, I know. I was just checking. At least now it's confirmed you don't care to speak to me or even offer the common decency to—*oh shit*." I lose my footing on the step as I go to sit on the lounge in the bathroom. "Wait... what was I saying?" I ask as I plop down on the cushion.

"Ava, where are you?"

"At school, genius. Where else would I be?"

"Have you taken something? Drank something?"

"I sure have, Dad, also ate some food. But you didn't ask that."

"Ava, what'd you take?"

I can hear some kind of shuffling, then an engine starting. "I took a Panadol."

"That's it? What'd you drink?"

"Why? Are you going to dob me in? No one likes a rat, Noah Hunt, no matter how pretty they are."

"You think I'm pretty? Actually, it doesn't matter. Where are you right now, Ava?"

"I'm in the girls' bathroom. But I gotta get to class. I shouldn't be talking to you, but it's nice to know you're not dead."

"Uh, thanks?" he says. "Ava, stay in that bathroom. Do not go to class, unless you want to get yourself suspended."

"I'm the good girl, Noah. You said so yourself. Good girls don't get suspended." I laugh.

"No, they don't. So be a good girl and keep your pretty little ass in that bathroom. I'm coming to get you."

"You can't come here. First, you're not a student anymore. Second, it's the girls' bathroom. You're not a girl. Are you?"

"Nope. But I'm coming to get you anyway. Just stay there." The phone cuts out. Did he hang up? Crap, I really shouldn't have had that third glass. My head is spinning now. I also should have eaten more.

Eat more; drink less. Next time.

Right now, I just want to close my eyes. Tipping my head back, I curl up on the sofa and rest my eyes. I'll just stay here for a moment. I'll get to class soon.

4

She's drunk at school. What the fuck was she thinking? Has she done this before? I press my foot down on the accelerator. Base is only ten minutes away from her school. I'm lucky I wasn't actually working, just training. I don't know what I'd do if I couldn't leave. Although, I'd take whatever punishment they fucking dished out, even if I had to go AWOL in order to help her.

It'd be worth it.

It would fuck up my plans, the very reason I'm back in Sydney to begin with. I have a six-month posting here until I complete the third stage of the special forces training program. I finished stage two a month ago. I think I needed a whole month to recover from that shit. It's hands down the hardest fucking thing I've ever had to face. Imagine every kind of deprivation, the sort no human should experience, and that's exactly what they put their candidates through. It's harsh. There's no room for weakness in the program. The next phase is eighteen months in Singleton, just a three-hour drive from Sydney.

From her. The fucked-up thing is, I can't tell her shit about what I'm doing.

Pulling right up to the school entrance, I jump out of my Jeep Wrangler and march up the steps. And just as I open the door, I'm stopped by the principal. "Mr Hunt, sir. It's a pleasure to see you again." He offers his hand for me to shake.

"Yeah, thanks." I'd like to say *I bet it's good to see me.* My family still donates a ton of money to this school.

"What can I do for you?" he asks.

Shit. "Jhett called. He's not feeling too good—kid's stuck in the bathroom. I'm just going to go drop him off some stuff. Won't be long." I walk straight past him like I own the place. I guess, in a way, my family probably does. Pulling my phone from my pocket, I text my cousin, telling him if anyone asks, he's not feeling well and I came by to help him out.

Then I realise I have no idea which bathroom Ava's in. I dial her number and it goes straight to voicemail. There are three bathrooms in the school. The first one I check is empty. Jogging down the hall, I turn the corner and run into the second one. I check all the stalls. And then, as I'm about to walk out, I see her. Curled up on the sofa that's tucked off in a little side room.

Kneeling down, I run my fingers through her long blonde hair. She's passed out. She looks so fucking peaceful. So fucking good. "Ava, baby, wake up." I lean down and kiss her forehead.

She swats at my face. "What? No, I don't wanna," she mumbles, not yet opening her eyes.

"Ava, babe, come on. I'll take you home so you can rest." I lift her so she's sitting upright, and she finally opens her eyes.

"Noah? What are you doing here?" She turns her head, taking in the empty bathroom.

"You called me. I told you I'd come get you. Come on." I grab her schoolbag, throw it over my shoulder, and pull her to her feet. She sways a little as she stands. "You okay? How much did you drink, babe?" The thought of her passed-out drunk at school, in a bathroom, so fucking vulnerable, pisses me the fuck off.

"Just three glasses. I'm okay."

"Let's go." I take her hand and lead her out one of

the side doors, walking around the building so I don't have to go back through the front entrance. I help Ava into the passenger seat of my Jeep, leaning over to buckle her seat belt.

"I can do that, you know," she says.

"I know, but so can I." I smirk, closing the door. For the second time, in as many days, I have Ava Williamson in my fucking car. She's quiet as I pull out of the school.

"I'm going to have to come back to get my car." She breaks the silence.

"Babe, you're not driving anywhere for the rest of the day. I'll get your car dropped off to you." In response, her stomach rumbles so loud I almost think an alien's gonna jump out of it. "Hungry? What have you eaten today, babe?"

"I had fruit." She looks away, digging into her bag that's sitting by her feet. She pulls out a bottle of water and swallows a huge gulp. It takes me fifteen minutes to pull into my building's carpark. "Where are we?"

"Home." I smile. It sounds good. I know I'm going to Hell for bringing a girl like Ava anywhere near my apartment.

"Home? As in, your place?"

"Yeah, come on." I get out, and by the time I make it around to her side of the door, she's already out of the car, her backpack tossed over her shoulders. I take her hand again and lead her to the elevator. Once inside, I press my finger on the screen and then we start our climb up to the penthouse.

"I should just go home. You really don't need to bother yourself with me. I'm sure you're busy." She looks me up and down. "Did you come from work?" she asks, noticing I'm still in uniform.

"Yeah."

"Oh shit, Noah, I'll get an Uber or something. Just... I'm sorry. I didn't mean to disturb your day."

I don't bother responding to her. The elevator doors open, and placing my palm at the small of her back, I walk her into my apartment and straight to the kitchen.

"Sit down," I instruct her, pointing at the counter before heading to the fridge. I pull out ingredients to make her a sandwich. She needs to fucking eat.

"What are you doing?" she asks, still standing at the counter.

"Sit down. I'm making you some food. You need to eat."

"I, um, I'm okay," she says, looking at the bread like it's going to attack her.

"No, you're not. You haven't eaten, and you've been day drinking. You need something in your stomach to soak up the alcohol."

"I... I can't eat bread," she blurts out, which pauses my hands as I'm about to spread butter on the bread.

"Why not? You allergic?" I ask, my eyebrows drawn in confusion.

"No, I'm a dancer. I have a strict diet, Noah. I don't eat carbs."

"Right, well, one sandwich is not going to kill you, babe. Trust me, I can always put you through a gruelling workout tomorrow to burn it off." Though the kind of work out I have in mind probably isn't what she's thinking. Placing ham, cheese, and a bit of salad on the sandwich, I cut it into triangles and set the plate on the bench. "Ava, sit down and eat," I tell her again.

"Argh, I'm only eating this because I'm actually really bloody hungry. Not because you're telling me to," she grumbles, finally lowering herself onto the stool.

"I don't care why you're eating it. I just care that you *are* eating it." I busy myself putting all the food back into the fridge. Then I hear it.

A moan. A goddamn fucking moan comes out of her mouth. I look back in her direction. She has her eyes closed as she chews. "Damn, I forgot how good bread was," she says around a mouthful.

My cock is instantly at fucking attention. She's eating a fucking sandwich, and I'm turned on. I have absolutely no hope of being around this girl and not ruining her.

"Are you sure your girlfriend isn't going to get upset that you brought me here?" The question comes out of left field.

I smirk at her, leaning my forearms on the counter

directly in front of her plate. "I don't know, babe. Are you upset that I brought you here?" I ask her.

"Um, no." She takes another bite of her sandwich.

"Then I don't think she's going to care." Straightening back up, I power on the coffee machine.

"So you do have a girlfriend then? Is that why you didn't text me back?"

"I do. She just doesn't know it yet. But she will. And no, I didn't text you back because you asked a stupid fucking question, Ava. Stupid questions don't get a response."

"What? No, I didn't. I asked how much I owed you. That's not a stupid question."

"It is when I have no intention of ever taking a single cent from you."

"You know, you're a little bossy, Noah."

"You want milk? Sugar?" I ask, pointing to the coffee machine.

"I don't drink caffeine." She shakes her head.

"How is caffeine any worse than the champagne you drank *at school*?" I emphasise the last bit.

"How did you know I drank champagne?"

"I could smell it on you." I don't tell her that I recognize the scent because it's what my mother smells like 24/7.

"Oh, sorry."

"Don't be. You want juice? Water?" I offer, instead of arguing about coffee.

"Water is fine."

I pour her a cup. Our fingers touch as she accepts the glass from me, and I swear I feel that spark again, the zap of energy that runs straight up my arm.

"Thanks."

I grab her empty plate and leave it in the sink. "Come on." Then I tug her up from the stool and take her hand. Opening the door to the theatre room, I flick on the lights. "Go and sit down. The remote is on the sofa. I'll be back."

"Where are you going?"

"To get changed. Go and find something to watch. You need to rest." Not waiting to hear her response, I walk out and head for my bedroom. I don't, however, miss her grumble something about a *bossy ass*.

I quickly jump in the shower to get clean. Okay, mostly to get clean, partly because I need to relieve my aching fucking cock. Lathering my hands with soap, I wrap one around my cock and lean the other against the wall of the shower. I slowly start to stroke up and down.

When I close my eyes, I can picture her. Standing in my kitchen, in that little fucking school uniform. A short blue and white checked skirt and a white button-up shirt. She's so fucking petite. Long, thin, tanned legs all on display. I imagine bending her over the bench, flicking her skirt up around her waist, and revealing that pert little ass of hers.

I picture spanking her. "Fuck me," I groan as I quicken my strokes, my grip firmer. I then envision pulling down her panties, burying my face into her pussy. My pussy.

Ropes of cum explode from my cock, and my knees buckle. Fucking hell, just the thought of her has me coming like a fucking fourteen-year-old kid seeing his first tit. I make quick work of washing off and dressing, throwing on a pair of gym shorts and a t-shirt.

I find Ava curled up on the sofa watching what looks to be a rom-com. I smile. As wrong as it is, it feels fucking right having her here. I go and sit down next to her, close enough that we're almost touching. "What are you watching?" I ask her.

She turns her head and looks at me. Then she sniffs the air. "You smell good. Did you shower?"

And there goes my fucking cock again, so much for relieving it. One look from her, one comment, and he's ready for more. "Yeah, I did."

"Here, it's your TV. You can watch whatever you want." She holds out the remote.

I take it and set it aside. "I want to watch whatever it is you're watching."

5

I should get up and go home. I always do what I should do. What's expected. But right now, all I want to do is sink into this sofa, curl up, and watch this movie. I want to bloody relax for once in my life.

Noah's arm wraps around my shoulders, before he effortlessly pulls my body up to his. He picks up a throw blanket with his other hand and lays it over me.

I'm engulfed by his peppermint scent. I let my head relax on his shoulder as his arm then snakes all the way around my waist.

Warm. Content. Those are the two words that pop into my mind as I feel my body sink into his. Then he brings his hand up from my midsection and starts combing it through my hair.

Cherished. That's a dangerous word. I don't want to be cherished by Noah Hunt, do I? Then his comments from earlier ring out in my mind.

Disgust. That word has me jolting to my feet. "I need to go."

"What? What's wrong?"

"*What's wrong*? Really, Noah? Not even half an hour ago, you told me you had a girlfriend and now you're lounging out on a sofa with your arms around me? I may not be very experienced at this sort of stuff. But I do know that if I was your girlfriend, I wouldn't be happy with the idea of you snuggling up with another girl."

He laughs, a sound so loud it drowns out the movie. "Babe, I told you there's a girl I consider to be my girlfriend. However, that girl doesn't know it yet."

"What does that even mean? How can you have a girlfriend if she doesn't know?" I don't get it. He's so damn confusing.

"Ava, it's you. You're *that girl*. I've been waiting years for you to acknowledge my existence. And I'll continue to wait. You might not be ready to accept that this..."

He points from himself to me. "...is happening. But we will happen. It's a matter of when, not if."

I'm speechless. Did Noah Hunt really just say he wanted me to be his girlfriend? That he's been waiting for me? What do I even say to that?

"You don't have to say anything. Come on, sit down and watch the movie. I'll take you home afterwards."

I let him pull me back onto the sofa and into his arms. Back where I want to be. My mind is reeling with everything that's happening.

Do I want to be Noah's girlfriend? How did he even know who I was? How long has he been waiting for me to notice him? Is he blind? How could he not see that I noticed him? He graduated two years ago, and I haven't seen him around since.

The Hunts are a well-known family. I'd often spot one of his cousins and wonder what happened to Noah. I considered asking once or twice and then thought better of it. What business was it of mine to know the whereabouts and doings of a complete stranger?

"Stop thinking so much, A. It will all be okay," Noah says, leaning down and kissing the top of my head.

I nod, take in a big breath, and try to switch off my thoughts. It's not easy. But eventually I feel myself sinking farther into his hold. Relaxing.

I must relax a little too much, because when I open my eyes again, it's dark. The movie screen is turned off and the room is quiet. However, it's so warm and comfy that I just want to shut my eyes and go back to sleep. Then I remember I'm not at home. *I need to get home.*

"Shit," I hiss as I unwrap the heavy arm from my waist and jump up.

Noah is on his feet in seconds, alert and scanning the room. "What's wrong? What happened?"

"I fell asleep. How long have I been out?" I ask as I feel around for my phone. Crap... twenty missed calls and thirty messages. "Oh God." I rush to put my shoes back on.

"A, slow down. It's okay."

"It's not okay. I should have been home two hours ago," I shriek.

"I'll take you home." Noah walks out of the room. I follow behind him, scrolling through my messages.

Mum: Are you coming home for dinner?

Dad: Where are you?

Mum: Call me back. Where are you?

Dad: Ava, call me back. Now. Or call your mother.

Ash: Ava, where the fuck are you? Mum and Dad are going out of their minds.

There are a few more from Ash, even one from Chase. Then there's one from Axel.

Axe: Ava, I've covered for you. Don't make me regret it. They all think you're studying in the library with Sophia. We're talking about this when you get home. I saw who you left school with.

Crap. I'm thankful for his help, but my little brother knowing I left school with Noah is not going to end well for me. Or Noah.

"What's wrong?" Noah turns around after he picks up his keys from the kitchen counter.

"Ah, my family is a little overprotective." I try to shrug it off.

"That's not a problem, A. That's a blessing."

"No, you don't understand. My brother saw me leave with you today."

Noah's eyebrows draw down. "Why would Ash be at your school?"

"Not Ash, Axel," I clarify.

And he laughs. "He's a sixteen-year-old kid, A. He's going to forget he saw anything by morning."

"Ah, no, he won't."

"Are you ashamed to be seen with me? Don't want your family to know about me?"

"It's not that. It's just... I've never had a boyfriend before, Noah. I've never taken a boy home. I've never even spoken about boys. And my dad and brothers think I'm a little princess, whose virtue needs saving at all costs."

Noah smiles, a huge grin that lights up his whole face.

"Why are you smiling? This isn't funny." I pick up my bag and throw it over my shoulder.

"You just called me your boyfriend. What's not to smile about?" Plucking the bag from my shoulder, he slings it over his own and takes hold of my hand. "Come on, let's get you home, before that virtue of yours really does need saving."

I can feel the blush rise up from my chest to my cheeks. Thank God he's in front of me and can't see it. Although, something tells me my virtue is indeed at risk around Noah. Because I'd willingly hand it over to him on a silver platter.

Noah pulls up in front of the house next door to mine as I instructed. Shit, what do I tell my parents about my car? I'll have to figure something out. I'm not good at this whole sneaking around thing. I've never had to do it before.

"Thank you for today." I unbuckle my seat belt and turn slightly to face Noah.

"You don't need to thank me, A. Tell your folks you didn't feel well so you had a friend drive you home. Your car will be fine in the school's parking lot overnight."

"Okay." Well, at least one of us can think of an easy lie. Though it's not really a lie, technically. I didn't feel well and a friend did drive me home.

I shift in my seat and pull the handle on the door. Noah reaches over and halts my movements. Turning my head back to face him, I watch as he slowly lowers his lips to mine. Stopping just before they touch. He's so close his breath warms my mouth. "Can I kiss you?"

Wait... he's asking me? Why is he asking me? Instead of answering him, I reach up and lock my wrists behind his head, pulling slightly until our mouths connect.

Noah's hand comes up and cups my cheek. His tongue darts out and parts my lips before he slips it into my mouth. He's not rushed. There is nothing sloppy or hasty about this kiss. It's slow, sensual. It's everything they write about in stories. This is the first kiss that will be permanently embedded in my memory. This is the kiss that will change my life forever. Whether it's for better or worse, I don't know yet. I just know that in this moment, right now, there is no going back.

From him.

Noah pulls away first, and I swear I hear myself whimper at the loss of contact. "I'll call you," he says.

Unable to form a coherent sentence, I nod my head and quickly jump out of the car. I don't look back as I run over to my gate and then up my driveway. The second I enter the foyer, the high of Noah's kiss evaporates.

"Where have you been? What's wrong with your phone?" Even though my dad's tone is tense, he wraps his arms around me and hugs me like he hasn't seen me in years.

"Sorry... it went flat. I was studying. Didn't Axe tell you?" I ask innocently.

"He did, but it's Axe. Unless I hear it from you, I can't be sure," he says.

"I'm sorry I made you and Mum worry. I'll take a charger with me in the future."

"Okay, come on. You're just in time for dinner. Ash is here."

I dump my bag on the floor near the stairs and follow my dad into the dining room.

"You're alive. You do know there's more to life than books?" Axe asks with a smirk.

"Yep, there's also dance," I retort.

"And boys." He coughs into his hand.

"Shut up. Ava isn't interested in boys, are you, sweetheart?" Ash adds with an intense glare.

"Boys? Nope. Definitely not boys." I smile as I walk over and hug my oldest brother. There is nothing *boyish* about Noah. He is all man. My man.

"Good. Keep it that way," Ash grunts in reply.

"Ava, how's the library? What were you studying?" This interrogation comes from my mum. "Tell me all about it as you help me in the kitchen." It wasn't a request, so I follow her out of the dining room. As soon as we're alone, she spins around on me. "Are you being safe?"

I'm stunned. Speechless. But quickly recover. "What?" I ask, honestly clueless.

"Don't be cute with me, Ava. I'm not in denial like

your father chooses to be. What's his name? And, again, are you being safe?" she presses.

"Don't worry, my virtue is still well and truly intact, Mum." I dodge her other question. I don't lie to my parents, and I really don't want to start now. "Can we just keep this between you and me?"

"Of course, I don't need your father leaving a trail of dead bodies all over the city." She laughs, although I'm not convinced it's a joke. If not my dad, then more than likely one of my crazy brothers or uncles would be up for the task.

"Okay, there is a guy. But it's new. Like very new."

"Is he from your school?"

"Ah, yep." Not a lie. Noah did go to my school, at one point.

"Okay, when you're ready to talk about this, I'm here. In the meantime, don't miss any of those daily pills." She winks, picking up a trayful of takeaway containers. I sigh in relief.

My mum is great at many things; cooking is not one of them.

6

Noah

My fingers grip the steering wheel. I'm silently listing all the reasons I had to let her walk into that house and not drag her back to my bed.

The main one being: she's still fucking seventeen.

I know she's eighteen in just two weeks' time. Just two more weeks and she's an adult. Technically, she's past the age of consent now, but something is telling me I need to keep myself in check until she's eighteen... at the very least. It really is up to her though.

Ava Williamson is my girlfriend. We agreed on that, didn't we? Maybe I should call her to confirm. No. That would be fucking pathetic and needy.

My phone rings through the car speaker. I look at the screen. Brent.

"What's up?" I ask my best friend. One of the only friends I've kept from my high school years.

"Meet me at Murphy's. I need a drink," he says.

"Now?"

"Yes, now, fucker. Hurry up."

"Okay, see you in a few."

Murphy's is a dive bar located on a backstreet in Kings Cross. We've been grabbing drinks there since before either of us was even eighteen—the legal drinking age.

Twenty minutes later, I walk into the bar and find Brent sitting in our regular booth. Looking at us, no one would ever think we would be best mates. We couldn't be more opposite if we tried. Where I'm all clean-cut, short back and sides, Brent is rough and unkept. Everyone gives him a wide berth as they pass the table. I don't know whether that's because of the scowl that's permanently imprinted on his face, or the leather cut he's sporting with the Vice President badge front and centre.

"Took you long enough. Where the fuck were you?"

he grunts, pushing a pint of beer across the table as I slide into the booth.

"Fuck off. I came, didn't I?"

"From where? Timbuktu?"

"Turramurra," I answer.

His whole face screws up. "What the fuck were you doing around there?"

"None of your fucking business. What's crawled up your ass and having you drag me out here anyway?"

"Can't a mate just want to grab a beer?"

"He can, but not you."

"Fine, if you must know, Cassidy is at the fucking clubhouse and I'm avoiding that like the fucking plague."

Cassidy, being the girl who's had the biggest crush on Brent for as long as I can remember. The feeling's never been mutual. He fucked her once, two months ago, and she hasn't let go since.

"Told you not to tap that. Knew after one look she'd be a stage-five clinger."

"A man can only resist fresh pussy for so long," he counters.

I raise my eyebrows. I'm no fucking saint but I'm the furthest thing from a slut. Unlike my mate here.

"Okay, you might be able to, but that's only 'cause you're all hung up on a girl you're never gonna have."

At the mention of Ava, I pull my phone out of my pocket and check the notifications. I was hoping she'd message me... about anything. The screen's blank so I place the device on the table.

"So why not just pick any other girl and take her back to the club? Send a message?"

"I did that last weekend. You wanna know what happened to Cindy the next day?"

"What?"

"Fuck if I know, because no one's seen her since. Vanished. Poof. Gone. But you know who isn't gone? Fucking Cassidy."

"Wait... you don't actually think little Cassidy had anything to do with this disappearance, do you?" I ask, unable to imagine the girl hurting a damn fly.

"Fucking oath, I do. That woman's fucking crazier than Satan himself." Brent makes a point of spanning his body with the sign of the cross. Like anything's going to save his ass from Hell.

"Okay, so you're fucked. Just put a ring on it and hope she doesn't get bored and kill you in your sleep," I deadpan.

"Right. Not happening. Ever."

"Hate to break it to you, but you can't get rid of her."

Cassidy happens to be one of his club members' daughters. He might outrank the old man, but club family is still family. Brent's father is the president of the Black Python's MC. It's the biggest one-percenter club here in Sydney.

"How's the training?"

I look around instead of answering him. He knows I'm training for the special forces program. I'm not stupid enough to open my mouth in a crowded bar about it, though. "How's your mum?" I ask.

"Good. She wanted to know when you're coming round for dinner."

"Soon. I've got shit to do." My phone vibrates on the table. I'm quick to swipe it up, but not quick enough.

"Get the fuck out of town. Spill now!" Brent hollers loud enough for all of fucking Sydney to hear.

"What are you on about?"

"Don't play dumb. It doesn't become you. Why the fuck is Ava Williamson texting you?"

"I gave her a ride home. She's probably just thanking me."

"Fuck off! You just *gave her a ride home*, the girl you've had a fucking boner for, for years. You expect me to believe that?"

"I don't give a shit what you believe," I say, absently opening the message.

Ava: Thanks again for the ride home and the movie. And the sandwich.

It's such a simple message, but she reached out. Which means she wants to talk to me. Why? I have no fucking idea, but I'm not going to argue with a fucking miracle.

Me: Anytime, babe. What time do you go to sleep?

I see the little dots pop up on the screen, as she reads the message, and wait for her reply.

"You know when you want to stop acting like a fucking teenage girl texting her BFF, I'll be here." Brent attempts to grab the phone from my hand. But the fucker's too slow.

"Touch my phone and I'll break your fucking hand," I tell him.

"You'd have to catch me first."

I raise an eyebrow at him. We both know I'm faster than his oversized ass. My phone beeps with a new message notification.

Ava: I have about sixty minutes of awake time left in me for the day. I have rehearsal at five tomorrow morning.

Me: Okay. Give me thirty minutes and I'll call you.

Ava: Why?

Why? Why do I want to call her?

Me: Because I want to.

It's as simple as that. Pocketing my phone, I down the remainder of my beer. "I gotta go. You need to go home or to the club. You can't avoid her forever."

"Tell me about it. So, what's little Ava up to? Still hot as fuck?" he asks as he pushes to his feet. And I push him back down into the seat. "Okay, okay!" he says, holding his hands up in surrender. "So, still hot as fuck—*got it*." He laughs.

"Fucker." I reach out and tug him up again. We

shake hands and part ways. Brent heads to his Harley while I head for my Jeep. I dial Ava's number as soon as I get off the elevator and walk into my apartment.

"Hello?" Her voice is quiet, almost like she's whispering.

"Hey, baby. How'd you cope with the interrogation?" I ask, assuming her family would have questioned the fuck out of her. Wondering where she was. Who she was with.

"Ah, it wasn't that bad. Axe is an ass but that's nothing new."

"And your folks? They're okay?"

"Yeah, well, my mum asked the name of the boy who kept me out."

"What'd you say?"

"That it's new and I'll tell her more when there's something to tell."

I don't know how I feel about that. I understand this is all *new* for Ava. But me? I've been waiting years for this.

"What'd you get up to tonight?"

"Ah, I met Brent at a bar, then came home to call you."

"What bar?"

"It's a dive bar. Trust me, babe, you don't know it."

"Will you take me there?"

"Fuck no," I answer.

"Oh, okay. Well, I should... um... I should go to

sleep. I have to get up early," she says, before cutting off the phone.

Shit. I hit redial but she doesn't answer. I send her a text instead.

Me: That's not what I meant, A. That bar isn't a place for a girl like you.

She reads the message, and seconds later her reply pops up on the screen.

Ava: What kind of girl am I?

Me: A good girl, A. My girl. Goodnight. I'll see you tomorrow.

She doesn't respond to that, but she doesn't have to. It's too late to turn back now—at least I fucking hope it is.

I'M WAITING at the front of her house. I've been here since 04:30. I pulled up just as her brother Axe was sneaking back in. He looked at me through the windscreen of my car, nodded his head, and walked through the gate. That kid is all kinds of trouble. I know because he hangs out with my little cousin, and I know what kind of trouble that shithead gets into.

Ava walks out at 04:45, tapping away on her phone. She doesn't notice me as I step out of the Lamborghini and open the passenger side door. "Need a ride?" I ask her.

She jumps, her hand goes to her heart, and her

glare lands on me. "Jesus Christ, Noah, are you trying to give me a heart attack? What the hell are you doing here?" she whispers, looking over her shoulder.

"Driving you to your dance club, obviously." My eyes have a mind of their own as they travel up and down her body. She's wearing one of those leotards with tights and a little skirt. Her feet are covered by a pair of UGGs, which makes me smile.

"It's a dance school, not a club," she says, stomping towards me. "And I've already called for an Uber."

"Cancel it. Get in, Ava," I tell her, nodding towards the car.

"And if I say no?" She folds her arms over her chest.

"Then I'll pick you up, throw you over my shoulder, and put you inside myself."

"You wouldn't dare," she says.

"Wouldn't I?"

We each size up the other for a minute before she caves and plops down on the passenger seat. "I'm only getting in because I'm already going to be late."

"Right." I shut the door and jog around to the driver's side. Once I've started the engine, I pick up the cup of green juice from the centre console and hand it to her. "Here, drink this. A green power smoothie: avocado, broccoli, spinach, mint, coconut water..." I stop when her face screws up. "It's good for you."

"I bet it is." She places it back down in the centre console without trying it.

"You know, I was up at four to make that just for

you?" I tell her. I see the guilt written all over her face as she picks up the cup and tentatively takes a sip. Seconds after the flavour hits her tongue, that guilt is replaced by surprise.

"Oh wow, it's good," she says. "Thank you. But you really shouldn't have gotten up so early to come and get me or make me smoothies."

"I was already up and I make those smoothies for myself. I just made extra today."

"So you guilt-tripped me into drinking your witch concoction?"

"Yep, you can't go and dance without having breakfast. I knew the chances of you actually eating a greasy bacon and egg roll were slim. So I made a smoothie instead."

"Thank you. And never bring me greasy food." She laughs.

"Deal. How long is rehearsal?" I ask her.

"An hour."

"I'll stick around and drive you to school." I calculate how much time I have. I can get her to school, go home, change, and then get to base.

"You don't have to do that."

"I want to." It's not a lie. "Can I watch?" I ask her.

"You want to watch me rehearse? It's going to be boring, Noah. You don't want to see that."

"Seeing you on a stage, babe, could never be boring."

"Okay, but I did warn you."

7

After my shower, I change into my school uniform and grab my bag. I find Noah waiting for me just outside the doors to the fitting room. He sat there for the whole hour and watched me dance up on that stage by myself. The entire time, I felt more alive than I ever have. Knowing that he was watching made me try harder, push myself further. I thought I'd be nervous with him there. I wasn't. It's almost like he was a comfort, which is odd. I don't really know him that well.

Seeing him now, I want to run up and jump on him, wrap my legs around his waist, and kiss him again. I wonder if he'd catch me.

I decide to live in the moment. Which is very unlike me. I drop my bag to the floor, run the couple of steps it takes to reach him, and leap into his embrace. He doesn't miss a beat, effortlessly catching me and wrapping his arms around my waist. My lips find his, and I instantly feel it. I thought it was all in my head last night, that I'd made it up. But it's real. I feel it now. It's an odd sensation. One that I'm not ready to let go of. One that I can't even label.

"Mmm," I moan into his mouth as our tongues intertwine. Noah grunts, takes three steps, and then my back is pushed up against the wall. I can feel his hardness as he grinds into my core. "Oh God!" It's like he's just ignited a spark within me. There are tingles all over my body.

"Fuck!" Noah growls, removing his mouth from mine. His lips then make their way down the side of my neck. His hands snake under my skirt and grab my ass.

My fingers wrap around the back of his head, the feel of his short, shaved military cut prickly beneath my touch. I arch my spine and grind my pelvis into him, my movements feverish as I try to reach the peak of the climb.

"Oh God, Noah!" My head falls to his shoulder, muffling my sounds into his shirt. Seconds later, I haven't just reached that peak. I'm tumbling over it blind. My whole body shakes and my panties are drenched. Shit. What the hell was that?

I've given myself orgasms before, but they've never felt like that. That was out of this world, and we're still fully clothed.

"Fucking beautiful," Noah says, tilting my head up and laying claim to my lips again.

He searches my face after a few minutes. "You okay?"

I smile, probably a dorky goofy smile, but I'm too high from that orgasm to even care. "I'm better than okay," I tell him.

"Good. Come on. Let's get you to school."

School... shit. I was meant to meet Sophia in the library at seven thirty. I'm going to be late. And that's becoming a bad habit when I'm with Noah. A habit I'm probably not going to break anytime soon.

Once I'm sitting in his car, I place my dance bag on the floor in front of me and pull out a spare pair of panties I packed. I'm not going to be wearing these wet ones at school all day. Not thinking anything of it, I shimmy the thin fabric down my thighs just as Noah gets into the driver's seat. His hands wrap around the steering wheel as he stares at me.

"Ava, babe, why the fuck are you taking your underwear off?" He grits his teeth like he's in pain.

"Because they're wet. I'm not wearing wet panties at school all day, Noah. Luckily I have spares." I hold up the black lacey pair I just removed from my bag.

"Jesus Christ, I'm going to Hell," Noah groans.

I get both feet through my clean underwear and am about to lift my hips off the seat to pull them up under my skirt, when Noah's hand reaches out and halts mine from moving the lace any farther up my legs.

"Stop. Wait a minute. There's only so much temptation a man can take, A. And knowing that your pussy is currently bare. In my car. Yeah, I can't let that happen and not get a taste," he says as he slowly trails his fingertips up the inside of my right thigh.

He watches my face as though he's waiting for my refusal. If he thinks I'm about to stop him, he's dreaming. I've never been more excited in my life. Anticipation runs through my veins. My breathing picks up in speed, and my heart is thumping in my chest. Then his fingers slide between my wet folds.

"Fuck me," he growls. Within seconds, his touch is gone as he holds his hand up at eye level. I can see my juices glistening in the sunlight. Noah then slowly licks up one side of his finger, his eyes closed as he sucks it between his lips. "Mmm, fucking perfection."

My mouth is gaped open. I'm so bloody turned on right now. I've never seen anything more erotic in my life. And dance, even ballet, can be extremely erotic.

"Put your panties on, babe, or we're never going to get you to school."

He expects me to just go to school after *that*? Is he mad?

I tug my underwear on, plug my seat belt in, and try my hardest to think about anything and everything else on the drive to school.

"You're not going to be drinking again today, are you? Is that like a regular thing for you?" he asks, sounding way more like my dad (or one of my brothers) than I'd like to imagine.

"Noah, I'm going to tell you this once and once only. I have a dad, a perfectly good one—no, a *great* one. I also have brothers, two to be exact, all of whom fit the very definition of overprotectiveness in the dictionary. Then there are my uncles and cousins... So, the last thing I need in my life is another overprotective male, trying to tell me how to live it."

"Ava, I'm only going to tell you this once, so listen carefully. I don't care how many brothers you have, and I'm fucking glad you have a great father. But I'm neither of those. I'm your boyfriend, who will always look out for you and want the best for you. So if I ask if you're going to be drinking at school, it's not to scold you. It's to know if I should be on standby to pick up your drunk ass. Also, if I do have to do that again, expect a lecture because you, babe, are way too fucking smart to waste that brain of yours by drinking your way through school."

I don't even know where to begin with that? "You're my boyfriend? When did we decide that?"

"Well, I decided two and a half years ago. You decided yesterday when you kissed me back." He smirks.

"I've kissed plenty of boys before you, Noah, none of whom ever ended up being my boyfriend." It's not until the words leave my mouth that I realise it was probably not something I should have said.

His eyes darken and his knuckles pale as he grips the steering wheel. "Ava, babe, do us all a favour and never mention the other guys you've kissed before. Ever."

I smile. "Well, if it makes you feel any better, you're the first guy to ever give me an orgasm."

His head shoots towards me so quick I fear it's going to snap off. "And the fucking last," he grits out.

"Eyes on the road, Noah." I wait until he's looking out the windscreen before continuing. "About this relationship thing, how much time does a boyfriend take up? Because I'm already stretched thin. Between school, dance, and my family, I don't really have a lot of time left."

"You're finished with school in six months, babe."

"And then I'm going to be a prima ballerina for The Australian Ballet."

"Without a doubt."

"So again, what sort of time commitment are we talking about here?"

"How about we just play it by ear... just see what happens." He pulls up right next to my car in the school parking lot. I see Sophia's hot-pink VW on the other side.

"Okay, well, thanks for the ride—again."

"Anytime, babe."

I open the door, and by the time I exit the spaceship that is this ridiculous car, he's around the hood and standing in front of me. "What are you doing?"

"Opening your door. Also, did you really think I'd let my girlfriend run off to school without a goodbye kiss?" He smirks as he looks me up and down. He doesn't give me time to answer before he has my knees buckling and my heart rate skyrocketing. Noah slowly pulls back, making no attempt to hide the way he adjusts himself in his pants.

"Does that hurt?" I ask, pointing to his boner.

"More than you know," he says.

"Oh, do you... do you want me to... help out with *that*?" I ask, unsure what I'd even do with it. I've never even seen one, let alone touched it.

He groans, "As much as I want to say yes to that offer, I'm going to take a rain check. I have to get to work, babe. See you later."

"Okay, spill the beans now, Ava Williamson. What the hell? When were you going to tell me you've been playing tonsil hockey with Noah Hunt?" Sophia squeals as soon as I open the door to our little study cave in the library.

"Shhh, jeez, you sure you don't want to take an ad out in The Sydney Herald?"

"Sorry, but what the what? I want deets. Yesterday, girlfriend. Tell me everything."

"Ah, there's really not much to tell. I met him the other night. He gave me a lift home. Then, yesterday, I drunk dialled him and he came and picked me up."

"And what? You slipped getting out of his car this morning and your tongue accidentally fell down his throat?"

"Something like that." I lift one shoulder in a shrug as I start pulling books out of my bag.

"Come on, Ava! I'm your best friend. If you can't tell me, then who can you tell?"

"Okay, he wants to be my boyfriend," I whisper. Like if I say it too loud, everyone will know.

"And you said yes, right? Please, for the love of God, tell me you said yes to that six-foot-whatever piece of deliciousness."

"I don't remember saying yes. But apparently he's taken to calling me his girlfriend anyway. But really, Soph, when am I meant to fit in a boyfriend? I barely have time to breathe most days."

"You need to make time for this, Ava. Don't let something we both know you've wanted for years just pass you by."

"I haven't wanted a boyfriend *ever*," I remind her.

"No, but two and a half years ago, when that boy was still at school, you wanted him. Don't even try to deny it."

"That was a long time ago."

"And now, you can have him. So just have fun with it. Don't take it so seriously. Don't go and create one of your plans or schedules for this, Ava. Just see what happens naturally."

That's twice within the hour I've been told the same thing: *Just see what happens.*

8

I t's been four fucking days since I've been able to touch her. I told her I'd be picking her up from school today, that I wanted to take her out. But now that I see her running towards me, all I want to do is take her home. Lie on the sofa, binge on bad food, and watch an awful rom-com.

We've talked every day. Morning, noon, and night. Texted back and forth between the calls. I don't think

I've ever had so much fun texting anyone before. She doesn't know it, but I've snuck into her dance school twice throughout the week. Both of our schedules were insane and it was the only way I could see her—even if briefly. It's now Friday night and all I want to do is keep her and never let her go again.

"Hi," she says, stopping just in front of me.

"Hi." I smile back at her. Opening the passenger door, I nod. "Get in, before I ravish the fuck out of you in front of all these teachers." I tilt my head towards the school building.

She quickly jumps into the Jeep. I know it's an eyesore, amongst all the Rolls and Bentleys pulling out of the school carpark. But this vehicle is as trusty as any of my sports cars. It also helps me fit in at base. No one there knows my true identity. I don't mention my family or how large my trust fund is. It's the one place I can truly be myself.

Once I'm seated next to Ava, I don't hold back. I take her face between my palms, pull her towards me, and slam my mouth over hers. "Fuck, I missed you," I murmur into her lips.

She giggles, and I swear I hear a fucking choir of angels. "It's only been four days, Noah."

"Four days too fucking long."

"Also, I know you came to watch me dance. So, technically, it hasn't been that long." She grins. And I pull away. *How the fuck does she know I was there?* There's no way she could have spotted me in the shadows. "It's a feeling I get when you're watching. I like it," she answers my unspoken question with a lift of her shoulder.

"Well, that's a good thing, because I fucking love watching you dance. I'd happily watch you up on that stage every day for the rest of our lives."

"That's a very long time." She smiles.

"Let's hope so." I don't correct her, knowing that for me, it might not be as long as she thinks. My career choice isn't exactly the safest.

"So, what are we doing? You have me until exactly 07:00 p.m. That's four hours. What are we going to do?"

"There is so much I could do to you in four hours," I say, letting my eyes roam up and down her body. "But we're not doing that. Did you bring a change of clothes?"

"Yep."

"Good, I'm taking you home first. You can change there, then we're going out."

"Where are we going?"

"It's a surprise."

"I don't like surprises. Hate them really."

"Nobody hates surprises," I tell her.

"Well, I'm not just anybody. I'm Ava Williamson and I hate surprises."

"You most certainly aren't just anybody. But trust me, babe, this is a surprise you'll like."

"How can you be so sure?"

"Because I know you, and I know what you like."

She drops the subject at that. Once we pull into my apartment building, she turns to me with a pouty face. "So, what's the surprise, Noah?"

"As cute as you are, I'm not telling you."

"Oh, come on! That pout works on everyone."

I laugh. "All that pout did was make my cock hard, thinking of how great it'd feel to slide it between those plump lips." Her mouth opens in shock, and fuck, if that doesn't make my cock harder. I use my finger to lift her jaw. Then, leaning in, I kiss her gently before pulling back. "Come on, the quicker you get changed, the quicker we can go.

"Okay."

~

I'm pretty sure I said we needed to be quick. Ava's been holed up in my bathroom for thirty minutes. What could she possibly be doing in there? "Babe, you okay?"

"Uh-huh, won't be much longer. Promise."

"Okay." I go and sit on the bed. Ten minutes later, I'm on my phone, rescheduling our booking when she walks out of the bathroom.

Fuck me. Gone is the young innocent schoolgirl I picked up this afternoon. In her place is a fucking gorgeous young woman. *An innocent young woman*, I remind myself.

She's wearing a black dress that sits halfway between her knees and hips. It's not short, but it's also not long. The material is tight, hugging her skin like a fucking glove. Her breasts, although petite, are perfectly sculpted by the fabric as it scoops up into a halter neck. My eyes roam down to her six-inch Valentino pumps. Then back up to her face—that fucking face. So fucking perfect. Dark eyes with bright-red lips. Her golden hair cascades in waves over one shoulder.

"Is this okay for whatever this surprise is?" she asks nervously.

"You look fucking edible, babe. Fuck, you look so fucking good. Maybe we should just stay in."

She laughs. "Not a chance. I did not just spend fifteen minutes rushing to get ready to stay in." It was more like forty minutes, but my intuition is telling me not to correct her on this one. Fuck, every fucking minute was worth it. Not that she isn't gorgeous naturally, without a spec of makeup on, because she is.

I stand and walk around her to turn the light off in my bathroom. My hands pause as I see all of her shit spread out over the counter.

"Oh, I'll clean that up," she says.

"Leave it. It can wait." The mess makes my skin crawl, and I feel like just going in there and packing it all away into the cabinets. But we need to head out.

"Are you sure? I'm sorry."

"It's fine, babe. Come on."

WE'RE an hour and a half late for the original booking by the time we pull up. Moving forward, I need to remember how long it takes Ava to get ready.

"We're going bowling?" she asks, looking around the carpark.

"Yep, I really hope you're as good as you say you are."

"Oh, you're so going down tonight, baby, because I don't lose. Ever." Her enthusiasm for winning is contagious.

"Well, *baby*. Tonight is going to be your first time." I emphasise the word *baby*. I watch her eyes widen and her breath quicken. "At losing," I add on. There's another first I'm dying to give her, but I'm patient. I've waited two and a half years for this girl. I can wait another week. I can wait until she's eighteen.

As IT TURNS OUT, she *is* as good as she claimed to be. I thought I was good. And I usually am, but have you ever tried ten-pin bowling with a raging fucking boner? It's not fucking easy. I was so distracted watching her tight little ass every time she bent over that I lost. *Badly.*

"I thought you said you could play?" she questions me as we hand our shoes over the counter.

"I can, usually."

"What's wrong? Are you sick?" She puts her hand up to my forehead to check my temperature.

"I'm not sick, babe." I take hold of her wrist, bringing it to my lips and kissing her palm. "Come on, I still have a whole hour before you turn into a pumpkin, right?"

"Right. You know, I can cancel my plans with the girls. It's nothing special. We just always use Ash's apartment for our slumber parties when he's out of town. It's stupid... Childish to be having slumber parties at our age. But we're all going off in different directions next year, and I guess we're making the most of what little time we have left together."

"It's not stupid. Nothing you do could ever be stupid. Well, maybe getting drunk at school wasn't your finest moment, but other than that..."

She slaps me across the arm. "It was one time."

"Meh, why don't you have your friends at our place? There's plenty of room there for everyone."

Ava looks at me blankly. "Our place? We don't have a *place*, Noah. I live with my parents. You have your apartment. There's no *our place*."

"My apartment is our place, babe. You just haven't moved in yet. That's all." I know I'm coming off too fucking strong, but fuck, if I don't want to steal her away and lock her in my castle.

Maybe I should just buy a fucking castle?

"Yeah, maybe let me finish high school first.

Because my dad would actually shoot you." Ava laughs.

"It'd be worth it." I lean over and kiss her. "So how about you change your party to the penthouse. I've got shit to do, so you'll have the place to yourselves most of the night."

"You want me to have my friends over, at your penthouse, and you won't even be there? Why?"

"Because I want you there. I like you being there."

"Okay... Let me send them your address."

I watch as she fires text after text to her friends. She then smiles and tucks her phone back into her bag. I raise an eyebrow in question. "So, they're coming to our place?"

"They're coming to *your* place, yes."

I don't correct her on the use of the wrong word again. I think if I say it enough, she'll start believing it.

I'VE SHOWERED AND CHANGED. I don't actually have plans, but I figured Ava would be more comfortable having her friends here if I wasn't hovering around them all night. I sent Brent a message to meet me at Murphy's. I'll stay away for a few hours and then come home.

To Ava.

I smile at the thought.

"Hey, Noah. Can I—oh." She stops in the bathroom and stares at the counter in confusion.

"Can you what, babe?" I ask her.

"Uh, what happened to all my stuff?"

"I put it away." I open the drawer then the cabinet, to show her all of her bottles, brushes, and packets of shit lined up neatly.

"I would have cleaned that up. You didn't have to do that."

"It's fine. You should just keep it all here anyway."

"Okay," she says quietly.

"What'd you want?"

"Oh, can I have your Wi-Fi password?" she asks.

"What for?"

"Really? You just moved all my cosmetics into your bathroom but give me the third degree over wanting the Wi-Fi password?"

"What devices are you using to log into the Wi-Fi?" I ask again, my tone serious. I may have no issue with her living here, but cyber-sharing is a whole other thing. I should get another router, have another line installed for her.

"I was just going to log in on my laptop, but it's okay. I can hotspot from my phone."

"No, it's fine. Just give me a minute and I'll set it up for you," I tell her.

"Are you sure? I don't mind using my phone."

"I'm sure, babe, just give me a sec." I lean in and kiss her.

"Okay." She turns and walks out the door.

Fuck, Ava's smart, and if she decides to go snooping around in my network files, which she could easily do with the fucking Wi-Fi password, she's going to see shit she shouldn't. She knows I'm in the Defence Force, but she cannot find out I'm training for the special forces.

I head into my office. Opening my laptop, I remove it from the home network system. It only takes a minute to do. I then crack the safe and place the computer inside. I'm not used to having other people in this house. I need to start being a little more careful with my security.

I find Ava in the living room, curled up on the couch, a book in her hand. "Babe, here you go. Just don't share it with anyone." I hand her a piece of paper with the Wi-Fi password. I'm changing it first thing tomorrow morning anyway.

"Thanks. Also, who the hell would I tell? The Russian spies next door?" She laughs.

"Funny." I sit down on the sofa and pull her into my lap. "I really love having you here."

"Well, I really love being here." She leans down and fuses her lips with mine.

Strawberries. How the hell does she always taste like strawberries? Whatever she painted on her lips hasn't budged a bit. It's a shame. She'd look hot as fuck with kiss-swollen lips and smeared lipstick.

"When will you be home?" she asks.

"I'm not sure. Don't wait up for me. Have fun with

your friends, Ava. I'm going to go before they all turn up. I'll see you later, babe." I don't actually make a move to leave. I have Ava fucking Williamson straddled across my lap. Where the fuck am I going?

"Where are you going anyway?" she asks, as if she can somehow read my thoughts.

"I'm meeting up with Brent. Remember Brenton Keller from school?"

"Uh-huh. I know who Brent is."

I pick her up and place her on the sofa as I stand. "I'll see you later, babe.

"Bye."

There's something on the tip of my tongue—three words that are desperate to come out. I don't say them though. Instead, I exit the apartment.

9

It's weird being in this apartment without Noah. I've only been here once before, and he's just left me alone. I can't help but snoop around a little. I have exactly thirty minutes before Sophia, Hannah, and Kia turn up.

I open random drawers and cabinets but find absolutely nothing of interest. Walking down the hallway, I stop at the door to what looks like an office. But I don't go inside. I turn in the opposite direction and head back to the living room. It's wrong to snoop. It's not my place to go digging through his stuff.

Oh God, what if there're cameras? I look up, my eyes skirting over every visible inch of ceiling. I don't see any cameras but that doesn't mean they're not there.

I find the control for his entertainment system, connect my cell to its Bluetooth, press play on my favourite playlist, and then sit back down and scroll through my phone.

I wonder what Noah could possibly have in common with Brent Keller? I know Brent joined his dad's MC. I've seen pictures of them in the papers. On the news. But I've never actually spoken to Brent. Noah isn't like that; he's not a criminal. He's not going to get mixed up in that lifestyle, is he?

No. He's too smart to go down that route. He's in the military. I have to remind my subconscious that he can take care of himself.

I'm about to send him a message when I'm saved by the shrill bell of a phone. It's the intercom by the elevator that leads into the apartment. "Hello," I answer.

"Miss Williamson. I have a Miss Sophia, Miss Hannah, and Miss Kia in the lobby wishing to see you," an older voice announces.

"Oh, sure. Send them up. Thank you." I need to

remember to ask Noah for his doorman's name. I should be thanking him by name.

"Very well," he says as he cuts the line.

Two minutes later, the doors of the elevator open and my friends, who appear to be in high spirits, spill out into the lobby. Sophia whistles. "Wow, I mean, Ash's apartment is nice and all, little dancer. But this, this is next-level nice." She spins around in a circle.

"Shut up," I tell her with a shove.

"She's not wrong," Hannah chimes in.

"This is opulence at its finest. You did well, little dancer. You scored yourself a Hunt," Kia adds.

"I didn't score myself an anything. And stop acting like you all don't come from old money." Every single one of them has a trust fund that could very well end starvation.

"Well, there's old money, and then there's Hunt money. You know, I've read the Hunts out-wealth the McKinleys."

"Really?" I ask, my eyebrows drawn together. The McKinleys are family—my Aunt Ella is married to Dean McKinley and they're super loaded.

"Yep. So where is he? This handsome mystery man of yours?" Hannah probes.

"He went out. We have the place to ourselves."

"Okay, let's get this party started then!" Sophia pulls out a bottle of champagne from her bag, effectively popping the cork and spilling the contents on the pristine white marble floors.

"Shit, Sophia, stop! Take that over there. I'm going to find a towel or something." I push her towards the kitchen. "And don't touch anything—or break anything."

"Psh, please, he's a guy. Like he'd know if anything got broken. Ash never notices."

"Ash doesn't say anything, but trust me, he notices. How do you think that vase you broke last time was replaced when I was there two weeks ago?"

"Huh? Maybe he thinks one of his floozies breaks all his shit," Hannah says.

"Ew." My brother and *his floozies* are the last thing I want to be thinking about. I run into the bathroom and grab a towel off the shelf. After I've mopped up the mess Sophia made in the foyer, I throw the towel into the hamper and find the girls sitting around the coffee table in the living room.

"Just in time, Ava! We're gonna play truth or dare."

I can't help but roll my eyes. "Don't you think we're getting a bit old for this game now?" I groan.

"We most certainly are, which only makes it more fun. Come on, you're up first. Truth or dare?"

Shit. If I choose truth, they're bound to ask me something about Noah, which I don't think I have answers for. Or at least not ones I'm willing to share with anyone. "Dare," I decide.

"Mmm, dare, okay. I dare you to sext Noah something," Kia shouts.

"What? No, I'm not doing that." I can feel the blush rise up my chest.

"Oh, you so are."

"What am I meant to sext him? I can't... I don't... I mean, we haven't..." I let my sentence drift off.

"You haven't *yet*, but you will."

Damn it. I pull out my phone. What the hell can I say to him that's sexy? I've never sent anyone a sexy message before. Noah and I have been texting each other all week, but it's never been anything but PG. My fingers start typing.

Me: Noah, I really like the feel of your lips on mine.

Nope, that's juvenile. Delete. I try again.

Me: Remember last week when you tasted me? Well, I think it's about time I got to taste you.

My finger hovers over the button. Can I really send this? What will he think of me? Nope, I can't do it. This is stupid. But before I can hit delete for a second time, Hannah reaches over and presses send.

"Shit, Hannah. Oh my God, I can't believe you did that! What's he going to..." My phone starts vibrating in my hand. "Shit, he's calling. What the hell do I do?" I ask, panicked.

"Answer it, duh." Sophia shrugs, as if that's helpful.

"Nope, I can't. We should just pack up our shit now. Let's go. We can stay at Ash's. I'm never going to be able to face Noah again."

"Don't be a drama queen," Hannah says.

The ringing stops and I sigh in relief, only to startle when it starts up again. Kia snatches the phone out of my hand and answers it. "Well, hello there, lover boy. This is Kia, Ava's very best of friends. She's otherwise indisposed at the moment, but I'll be sure to get her to return your call ASAP."

Shit, I can't do anything but watch the train wreck that has become my life. I have no idea what Noah is telling Kia, but she nods her head and then shoves the phone back in my direction.

"It seems lover boy is very keen to talk to you, little dancer." I look at the device like it's going to jump out and attack me.

"Argh. I hate you all," I hiss at them before I grab the phone, stand, and stalk out of the living room. "Hello." My voice comes out a little more timid and unsure than I'd like it to.

"Babe? Everything okay?" Noah asks.

"Uh-huh. Fine. Dandy. What could possibly be wrong right now?" I blabber.

"Well, how about the fact I'm standing in the middle of a fucking dive bar with a raging boner because someone just put a certain image into my head."

"Oh, well, I guess that could be a problem. For you," I tell him.

"Ava, you know I'd never make you do anything you don't want to do. I don't need you to push yourself before you're ready to do anything. Like that."

"I, well, I guess."

"Ava, go back to your friends, babe. I'll see you later. Unless you need me to come home now?"

"Ah, well, I personally would love for you to come home, but I do fear for your safety if these girls get their claws in you."

"I think I can take 'em."

"Mhmm." I know I need to hang up. There's that awkward silence where I want to say something, but I can't get the words out. "Noah?"

"Yeah?"

"I... I really like you." And I know I sound like an idiot.

"Well, thank fuck for that, because I really fucking like you too, A." He hangs up, and I go back into the living room to face the girls.

"So, what'd lover boy want? Wondering if you're gonna deliver on that promise of yours?" Hannah asks.

"Shut up. We are never playing that game again. Let's just go pick a movie or something trashy to watch. I'm exhausted."

We spend the rest of the night in Noah's theatre room, watching reality TV shows and judging the rich and famous. The night is filled with laughter, gossip, and absolutely no more talk of Noah Hunt.

I FEEL MYSELF BEING LIFTED. My head falls against a solid brick wall. No, it's not a wall; it's a chest. A solid chest. My eyes blink open.

"Noah?" I ask. The room is dark, but I know it's him. I know by his touch, by the cinnamon and whisky scent that is somehow uniquely *him*.

"Yeah, babe, shh. I'm taking you to bed. You're not sleeping on a fucking sofa," he says.

Is he mad? He sounds mad. Shit, did we make too much of a mess? Eat too much food? Well, I know I didn't... but the other girls sure as hell made themselves at home.

I let my head relax on his chest. And the next thing I know, I'm being placed on a bed. I open my eyes to find Noah digging through a set of drawers. Shit, I'm in Noah's bed. Oh God, am I ready for this?

I think I'm ready for this.

Then I watch as he pulls his shirt over his head, revealing his back. A very muscley, toned back. Yep, I'm so ready for this.

Noah turns around and struts towards the bed. "Sit," he says, pulling me upright. He places a shirt on top of the sheets and tugs me to my feet.

He reaches up and undoes the front of my dress, then finds the zipper on the side and slides it down. The dress falls to the ground, pooling around my feet. Leaving me standing in front of Noah in nothing but a pair of black lace panties.

"Fuck me. You're so fucking gorgeous. Shit. Here."

He reaches behind me and tosses the shirt over my head. My arms automatically slide into the sleeves.

What is happening here? Why is he dressing me... right after getting me undressed? Does he not want me like that? Have I read this whole thing wrong? Surely not.

"As much as I want to take everything right now, A, I'm not going to. We're waiting. One week and you'll be eighteen. We just have to wait a few more days."

"What if I don't want to wait?" I pout. I mean, I don't mind waiting. But really? Don't I get a say in this?

"You don't want to wait? Tough. I'm waiting. I'm trying really fucking hard to do the right thing here, Ava."

"But we can do other things, right? I mean, we don't have to do... *it*. There are other options?" I ask him, and I have no idea where that confidence comes from.

10

But we can do other things, right?

Fuck me, I was doing everything I fucking could to control my dick. Having her in my room. In my bed. But with those words, I've lost any little control I thought I had.

"That depends." I smirk.

"On what?" she asks, blinking up at me. Fuck, she's so fucking pretty. She's washed all traces of makeup off her face, and I think I like this look so much more. She's fucking pure innocence. Peering up at me. Waiting for me to take the lead. She should be running out the door. Not putting all this trust into being alone in a bedroom with me.

"Have you been a good girl tonight, Ava?"

"I'm always the good girl, Noah. How about you make me the not-so-good girl?" Her hands fall to my bare chest.

"Mmm, as tempting as that is, I like you better good."

"It's a good thing I'm always good then."

My lips slam onto hers. I fucking love kissing this girl. I can't get enough of her. She jumps up and wraps her legs around my waist. Lifting her from my body, I throw her down onto the bed. She lands in the middle, her golden hair sprawled out around her like a fucking halo.

"I'm going to have fun with this body of yours, baby. Do you want that? Do you want me to make you feel good?"

She nods her head.

"I'm going to need the words, babe. Do you want my mouth, my hands, my fingers all over you?" I ask as I tug up the same shirt I just pulled down moments ago, baring her smooth flat stomach.

"Yes. Please, Noah, please." She squirms under the light touch of my fingertips as I yank the shirt all the way over her head. Her breasts are bare, small, and pert. Enough to fill my palms perfectly. Her nipples taunt. My mouth goes straight for its target. Sucking. Nibbling. As I cup her breasts. "Oh God, that feels so good. Why does that feel sooo good?" Ava moans as her spine arches upwards at what appears to be a very unnatural angle.

I release her breast with a pop. "Babe, you're going to fucking break your back if you keep bending it like that." I flatten my hand along the middle of her chest and push her down into the mattress.

"I'm very flexible, Noah. I'm a ballerina, you know."

Images of all the ways I want to test out just how *flexible* she is run through my mind. Fuck. "We're going to have so much fun testing that theory. But not tonight." I kiss my way down her stomach until I get to the top of her underwear.

I look up and our eyes connect as I slowly drag her panties down her legs. She doesn't waver when I spread her thighs. She keeps her eyes locked on mine, a look of pure curiosity and need evident on her face. I trail my tongue from her left knee all the way up, stopping just as I reach the lips of her pussy. I lift her right leg and repeat the process.

Ava tilts her pelvis towards my face. I smirk into her inner thigh. "You want something in particular, baby?" I ask her. Her face reddens and she closes her eyes. "Ava, open your eyes." My voice is firm. Hard. And her lashes snap open with the command. "Tell me... what do you want me to do while I'm down here at heaven's doorstep?"

"Ah, I don't know," she whispers.

"Yes you do. Tell me, Ava. What do you want?" I urge her, pushing her past her comfort zone. After all, she's plenty comfortable being spread out naked on my bed, but she's too shy to ask for what she wants. By the time I'm finished with this girl, she's going to have more confidence than fucking Superman. Who am I kidding? I'm never going to be finished with her.

"I-I want you to, you know. Use your tongue. Down there."

"You want me to eat out this sweet-as-fuck pussy of yours?" I ask as I slide a single finger through her bare, wet folds.

"Oh God, y-yes." Her voice shakes.

"Well, since you asked so nicely," I say, right before I let my tongue sweep up from her ass to her clit. I'm in no rush. I repeat the process slowly. Circling and nibbling on her clit when I reach it. I really could stay down here all fucking night.

"Oh God. Noah," Ava screams.

I pick up the speed and increase the pressure of my tongue as I flatten it out. Before I gradually insert one finger in her tight pussy, stopping when I hit the wall of innocence that's still very much intact. Fuck, I want to ram my dick through that wall.

My teeth graze her hardened nub and she deto-nates, her whole body seizing. I continue licking her until she's come back down. Then I crawl up her much smaller frame and claim her mouth. She wraps her legs around my waist and grinds herself on my cock.

"Fuck, babe, we need to stop before I lose all common sense." I straighten, removing her legs from around me. I grab the shirt and throw it over her head as she pops her arms through the sleeves and tugs it down over her body. "We, ah, we should get some sleep, babe," I tell her, pulling the blankets back.

She looks up at me with that fucking pout of hers. The exact one I want to shove my cock through. "Noah? Do you... can I help you out with that?" she says, pointing at the very obvious boner trying to rip through the fabric of my jeans.

"You don't have to do that, Ava. Come on, get in." I nod to the top of the bed. She crawls up and rests her head on the pillow. Removing my jeans, I leave my briefs on and climb in next to her. We lay there, facing each other.

"I know I don't have to. But can I?" Ava whispers as her tiny, delicate hand travels down my chest and over the ridges of my abs.

"Fuck, babe, you're killing me here."

"Please?" She bites on her lower lip as her hand dips under the band of my briefs and wraps around my cock.

"Are you sure you want to do this? I mean, you know I don't expect you to, right?"

"I'm sure. Just tell me what to do. I haven't..." She looks down and doesn't finish her sentence.

I tilt her chin up. "Babe, I fucking love that you haven't done these things before, that I'll be your first and last everything." I wrap a hand around hers. "Tighten your grip, and stroke. There's really not much to it." I move my palm up and down with hers a few times before I let go and allow her to take control.

Her hands are smooth, silky. "Do they all feel this soft?" she asks me, and I can't help but smile.

"I don't know, Ava. I don't make a habit of feeling other guys' dicks."

"Huh, maybe I should touch some others to find out," she murmurs.

I freeze. "If you touch another guy's cock, I will fucking rip it off him," I tell her. "You and me? This is as exclusive as it gets. There's no one else. Ever."

"Okay. I was joking." She smiles.

"Joking about touching some other guy's dick is not funny."

"Got it." She continues to smirk before she rolls over to her stomach and starts ducking under the covers.

"What?" Oh shit. Fuck me. She's just licked up the underside of my cock, then circled her tongue around my tip. She's really taking to this exploring thing well. "Oh God, shit, babe," I hiss as she sucks me into her mouth.

"What? Did I do it wrong?" she asks, peering up at me.

"Fuck no! Your mouth feels fucking amazing. There really is no wrong way to do this. Just no teeth. Don't bite."

"Okay," she says and dips her head back down. She takes me a little deeper, keeping one hand wrapped around the base of my cock. She's a fucking natural, hollowing out her cheeks as she comes up off my cock before sliding back down again.

I'm not going to last much longer like this. "Ava, baby, I'm going to come." I pull on her arm to drag her off but she doesn't budge. "Fuck. Shit..." I explode into her mouth.

She fucking swallows it. Well, most of it. There's a bit on the side of her lip and some on my cock. But fuck me, she swallowed. She wipes at her mouth. "That's surprising... Not anywhere as bad as I thought it would be," she says.

"Are you okay? I tried to warn you. To get you up."

"Why?"

"So I didn't come down your throat. Come here." I pull her towards me and wrap an arm around her waist. Her head rests on my chest.

"Was it good? I mean, I know I'm not any good at this sex stuff, but was it okay?"

"Ava, you are fucking amazing. Perfect in every way. Never doubt yourself, babe."

"Okay."

"It's late. Let's get some sleep." I reach over and turn off the bedside lamp. We lay there in the darkness. In silence. I couldn't be more fucking satisfied if I tried. It feels fucking right, having her here in my arms. I have no fucking idea how I'm going to let her go tomorrow. "What are your plans for your birthday next weekend?" I ask her.

"Ah, I have a family dinner thing on Friday night, then I'm meant to be meeting Sophia. She wants to go hit up every nightclub."

"What do you want to do?" I ask her.

"Nightclubs aren't really my thing. I mean, I like Ash's club. But let's be honest, whatever I do there will get back to my brother."

"Mmm, maybe you and Sophia should just go to Ash's club for the night."

"Pass."

"How much will your folks worry if you disappeared for the weekend?" I ask her. I want to take her away. I want to spend more than a few hours with her.

"Um, they'll be fine. I'll just tell them I'm going away with a friend."

"Do that. I'll pick you up Friday night from whatever club you and Sophia end up at."

"Mmm, okay. Noah?"

"Yeah?"

"I like you."

I lean down and kiss her forehead. "I like you too, babe."

11

"Happy birthday, dearest Ava. Happy birthday to you." My whole family sings off-key as I stare at the massive three-tier chocolate cake I have no intention of eating.

"Blow out your candles and make a wish, baby," my mum says. She's smiling so wide any onlooker would think it was *her* birthday.

I run through all the wishes I could make, but there

is only one that lingers. I think of Noah, close my eyes, and blow out the candles. I can't believe I'm officially an adult today. I'm eighteen. I can vote. I can drink —legally.

I've only seen Noah twice this week. The longer we spend apart, the more I find myself missing him. I knew it would be like this, though. My schedule is crazy busy and so is his. The little time I do get to sneak away and just be with him, those are the moments when I'm most at peace. When I'm most relaxed. And if I'm being honest, when I'm with Noah, I'm more myself than I ever have been before.

"So, what'd you wish for?" my cousin, Hope, asks. "A new car? Bag?"

"Neither, and I'm not telling you. If I tell you, it won't come true." I sip on the glass of champagne I'm clutching as if it were a lifeline.

"Come on, I won't tell anyone."

"Never!" I shake my head.

"Leave her alone, Hope. Sweetheart, I have to go into the club. What are your plans tonight?" Ash turns to me and asks.

"I'm meeting up with Sophie. She has some clubs in mind."

The expression that takes over Ash's face appears pained. "Fuck. Hang on, let me get Chase to go with you girls." He pulls out his phone.

Chase is my brother's best friend. However, he used to live with us when they were still in high school so he's kind of like an adopted brother. An adopted brother I don't need hovering over me all night.

"Nope, not happening, Ash. No way."

"What's not happening?" Axe butts in.

"Ash is being an ass." I literally stomp my foot.

"What's new?" Axe shrugs.

"Fuck off. Ava wants to go out clubbing with Sophia. All I wanted was to send Chase with them."

"You sure you want to go clubbing? What's that boyfriend of yours going to think when a bunch of slimy men are grinding all up on you?"

"What fucking boyfriend?" Ash folds his arms over his chest.

"There is no boyfriend." I glare at Axe and he laughs.

"Right, my mistake." He walks away, shaking his head and typing something on his phone.

"Ava, why don't I reserve a VIP table for you at The Merge?" My big brother looks like he's going to burst a vein in his forehead from the stress.

"Ash, I worry about you. You need to relax or you're going to give yourself a heart attack before you're thirty, and you're not leaving me alone with Axe."

"Fine. But I want you to call me the minute you enter and leave each of the clubs. I want to know where you are, at all times, Ava," he grunts.

"You might look like Dad, but you're not him." I smirk and walk in the opposite direction before he ends up getting his way. Ash has the uncanny ability to somehow get things done exactly how he wants them.

"Okay, where are we going tonight, little cousin?" Hope asks.

Shit, what is it with my family? Have they always been this overbearing and I just didn't notice? Or is it only now, when I want to be able to sneak away with Noah at the end of the night?

I have my overnight bag already packed in the car. My stomach is turning with butterflies, though I can't tell if it's from excitement or nerves. "Ah, Hope. I love you—you know I do. But I made plans with Sophia tonight, for just the two of us. How about next weekend we all go and drink Ash out of business?" I suggest.

"Deal. Have fun tonight, Ava. But not too much fun."

"Thank you."

"Ava, come with us. Mum and I have something for you," My dad calls me over, and I follow him into his office.

"Oh my gosh, I'm so excited. I've been itching to show you this for months," my mum squeals.

"Now, Ava, sweetheart, just because we're giving you this does not mean you're moving out. And it doesn't mean we don't expect you here every night," my dad says in his stern, *don't argue with me* voice.

"Zac, stop it. Show her already," Mum scolds.

Dad screws up his face and then hands me a folder.

I open it and a plastic card falls to the ground. There's a flyer for an apartment inside.

"What is this?" I ask confused, picking up the card.

"We bought you an apartment close to the dance school. For those nights when you have late rehearsals, so you don't have to drive all the way here."

"You bought me an apartment?" I ask.

"Yep, Aunt Rye and I have already furnished and decorated it for you." Well shit, if my Aunt Rye had a say, I know it must have cost my dad a pretty penny. Aunt Reilly is my Uncle Bray's wife; she's known for her expensive taste and great style.

"I don't know what to say?" I'm speechless. I thought my dad would try to keep me here until I was thirty.

"Like I said, this is not you moving out, Ava. This is you having somewhere safe to sleep when you need it," Dad clarifies for the second time.

I wrap my arms around him. "Thanks, Dad. This is amazing. I promise I'm never leaving." And we both know that's a lie, though one of us may be in denial.

"Good." He kisses the top of my head. "How the fuck are you eighteen already?" he asks.

"Language," my mum says. Dad and I laugh. She has been trying to get my dad and my uncles to watch their language around us kids for as long as I can remember. You'd think she'd give up by now.

There's a knock at the door. I glance over and see that Joshua McKinley stands there, as stern and scary as ever. Josh is what I like to call *frenemies* with my dad. It's complicated, but they have to play nice, considering my dad's sister is married to Josh's brother. And my cousin, Dominic, is their shared nephew. Josh may be intimidating to anyone outside the family unit, but to me, he's never been anything but the fun uncle who knows how to give really good gifts.

"Ava, got a moment? I have a little something for you," he says.

Dad groans loud enough for the whole house to hear.

"Sure. Thank you again. Mum, Dad, best gift ever!" I hug both of my parents. "Also, don't wait up for me. I'm going to spend the weekend with Sophia."

My mum gives me a knowing look. Shit, she can tell I'm lying. I should probably just tell them about Noah. But I'm not ready for that. I don't think my dad is ready either.

"Okay, have fun, sweetheart, but not too much." *Why does everyone keep saying that?* "You still got that can of mace in your bag?" Dad asks.

I roll my eyes. Thinking back on it, that can of mace might have come in handy a few weeks ago when that slimeball had me pinned up against my car. I nod my head and follow Josh out to the front of the house. My steps falter when I see the shiny white Mercedes SUV sitting in the driveway with a huge pink bow on top.

"What?" I look around, but it's only me and Josh out here.

"Happy birthday, Ava." He holds out a set of keys.

"You bought me a car? Seriously? Oh my gosh." I hug him. He's not a fan of people touching him, unless it's his wife or daughter. But I don't care. He just bought me a car. A really bloody nice car. "Thank you, thank you, thank you."

"You're welcome, sweetheart." My uncle returns my hug, squeezing me tight. "I don't understand why all you girls have to get so grown up."

"Aw, don't worry, Josh. I'm sure Bree will give you little granddaughters to spoil before you know it."

His whole body stiffens at the mention of his daughter. And if looks could kill, I'd be dead. In fact, I'm sure he's thinking of all the ways he can dispose of my body right now. "That's not even remotely funny, Ava," he grumbles. "Don't drink and drive. I'll confiscate the car if you do." He smirks and turns to walk inside.

"I would never do that," I say to his retreating back. Pressing the button to unlock the car, I squeal as I jump in the driver's seat and look around. I love this. He somehow upholstered the interior with pink leather.

The passenger side door opens and Axe jumps in. "Nice wheels," he says.

"Yep, get out!" I glare at him.

"Nope, you're giving me a ride into town."

"Ah, no, I'm not. I'm picking up Sophia and we're going out. You can catch an Uber."

"Really? Should I go and tell Dad you want your baby brother to catch public transport, instead of giving him a lift?"

The little shit. Our dad has this thing about us catching public transport. His parents were killed during a mugging at a train station when he was younger. He had to raise my Uncle Bray and Aunt Ella on his own.

"Fine, but wait here and don't touch anything," I tell him. Running over to my Beamer, I grab my suitcase from the boot and struggle to lift it into the SUV. "A little help would be great, Axe."

He jumps out and effortlessly plops my bag into the back of the car. "What the hell are you packing for?"

"I'm staying with Sophia this weekend," I maintain my lie.

"I'm sure you are," he says under his breath while shaking his head. He rips the bow off the bonnet of the Mercedes before jumping back into the passenger seat.

I pull out of the driveway. "Where am I taking you?" I ask.

"Jhett's. Here, I'll type in the address."

"Jhett Hunt?" I ask, "As in Noah's cousin, Jhett?"

"That's the one. Why?"

"No reason. I didn't realise you two were friends."

"We're not. But when my sister started to sneak around with his cousin, I made it a point to befriend him. You know, there're a lot of nasty fucking skeletons in the Hunt family closet, Ava."

"I'm not sneaking around with anyone." Deny, deny, deny.

"And the tooth fairy is real too. I'm not an idiot. We go to the same fucking school. Do you really think no one has seen you getting in or out of his car?"

"Wait, are people talking about me at school?" I ask. I've never been the topic of the rumour mill. Ever. And I don't intend to be now.

"No, some jock tried to say shit about you in the locker room. Don't worry, I made sure no one would make that mistake again," he says.

"Axe, don't get into fights for me."

"Why the fuck not? Fighting for you is the most noble of reasons to fucking fight. You're the only reason I learnt to fight in the first place. I knew you'd grow up to be too fucking pretty and attract the attention of boys." He shrugs.

"I don't attract the attention of boys," I argue.

"You do. You've just never noticed until Noah fucking Hunt came snooping around. You know Dad and Ash are going to burst a vessel when they find out about this boyfriend of yours. Especially when they realize how much older he is."

"If you're so sure that Noah is my boyfriend, then why aren't *you* bursting a vessel? And he's not that much older."

"Because I haven't seen you this happy or relaxed

in a long fucking time, Ava. You deserve to have some fun. SOME. You've always been way too high-strung. But if he hurts you, or touches you in any way you don't want, I will fucking kill him."

"Oh, you don't have to worry about that. I very much like the way Noah touches me." I smirk.

Axe's face screws up. "Maybe I'll kill him just for the hell of it. It's not too late for you to follow Jesus. I'm sure Uncle Bray will help get you into a nunnery."

Technically, it's not too late, but it will be after tonight. I decide to keep that bit of information to myself. We pull up at one of the many Hunt family estates. "Axe, thank you." I hug him. I know we might give each other shit, but he really is the best little brother a girl could ask for.

"Anything for you, Ava. Just don't be stupid. And call me if you need me." He jumps out of the car and runs up to the intercom. Seconds later, the black iron gates swing open and I watch as he jogs up the long, winding driveway.

12

I've been watching Ava from a distance for the last ten minutes as she laughs and dances with her friend, Sophia. I told her I'd wait for her to call me to come and pick her up. And I know she needed this experience with her friend, but fuck, every fucking guy within a ten-kilometre radius has his grubby eyes on her.

So, yeah, I told her I'd wait, and I'm fucking trying

here. It's like there's an animal instinct clawing at my insides, urging me to go and mark my territory, because that girl is fucking mine.

I watch her drag Sophia off the dance floor and head for the bar. She's been drinking water all night, which surprises the hell out of me. Most fresh eighteen-year-olds would be out drinking themselves into a coma on their birthdays. Not Ava. She's far too responsible for that. She's always thinking ahead and never just for the moment.

Once they get their drinks, the girls move over to a booth. Within seconds, the fucking vultures are making their rounds. As two fucks in way-too-tight jeans stop at their table, I start making my way over. It's time to stake my fucking claim. Ava seems nervous. She's looking around the club as though she's searching for the exit.

"Babe, sorry I'm late. Traffic was a bitch," I say, wrapping my arms around her. My lips are quick to find hers. And the moment they touch, all that pent-up animalistic energy simmers down. Pulling away, I bury my face into her neck. "Happy birthday, A. How's it feel to be an adult?" I ask into her ear. I lift my head and I'm met by her beaming smile.

"A hell of a lot better now that you're here."

My heart soars at her response, at the smile on her face. I can't wait to get her out of this club and have her all to myself.

Sophia reaches over the table and taps Ava on the

arm, pulling her attention away from me. She nods her head in the direction of the door. Ava follows her gaze, and her eyes widen before she instantly stands and marches in that direction.

I follow her because, well, because I don't fucking know how not to. I'm two steps behind her when she stops and pushes on some guy's chest. I don't catch what she says to him, but I'm quick to wrap my arms around her waist when she goes to shove at him again.

The guy—*kid* really, because he looks fucking young—glares at me. The smile he just had on his face disappears as he clenches his jaw and closes his fist.

"Dom, no. Don't even think about it." Ava takes hold of his hand and walks out of the club. And what do I do? Fucking follow her, of course.

"What the fuck, Ava. Who the fuck is this?" the guy, Dom, questions.

I slip an arm over Ava's shoulder. She looks up at me. "Not helping, Noah," she hisses before she turns her attention back to the kid. "What the hell are you doing here, Dom? How'd you even get in?"

The kid ignores her, choosing to send daggers my way instead. "You have three seconds to remove your hand from my cousin before I remove it from your fucking body." His words are spoken in a calm, even tone. His eyes are void of all emotion. And I have no doubt he'd actually try to deliver on his threat.

I smirk. At least I now know who the fucker is.

Dominic McKinley. A rich, spoilt-over, privileged kid. "You're welcome to try," I tell him.

"Nope. No, you're not. Maybe I should call Aunt Ella and see what she thinks of you being here?" Ava pulls out her phone.

"Go ahead. Maybe I'll put a video chat through to Uncle Zac, Uncle Bray, Ash—I'll even add my dad and Uncle Josh just for good measure, Ava."

"You wouldn't dare," she seethes at him.

"Are you sure about that?" he retorts, drawing his own device from his pocket.

Fuck me. Something tells me the Williamsons/McKinleys are nothing like my family. If either of them puts their call through, I'm sure the whole lot will be here within minutes.

"How about we head out? We can give your cousin a ride home?" I suggest to Ava.

"Good idea. Follow me. And, Dom, don't even think about arguing, because if you do, I'm telling Josh it was you who tripped Breanna that one time and made her get a black eye."

I've never seen a kid's face pale so quickly. "That was when we were like eight, Ava."

"Yeah, I don't think Josh will really care how much time has passed." Ava shrugs.

Fuck, she's ruthless.

"Fine, I'll let you drop me home. But don't think for a minute that your little secret boyfriend here is safe." He glares at me.

Ava ignores him, places her hand firmly in mine, and pulls me up the road. I look to Sophia, who isn't far behind us, and she just laughs. "Don't worry, Noah, they're always like this."

Right... I wouldn't know. My family is so fucked up I don't really have a reference for normal. I get along fine with my cousin, Jhett. But other than that, I wouldn't lose sleep if any of them stepped on a minefield.

Ava stops at a white Mercedes SUV. She digs keys out of her little bag and presses a button. I hold out my hand. "I'll drive," I tell her.

"Ah, no, you won't. I just got this baby today. You are so not driving it." She walks around to the driver's side, leaving me standing on the footpath.

I jump in next to her while Sophia pushes Dominic through the side door. "Little dancer, can you drop me off at The Merge," Sophia calls from the back seat once Ava pulls out into traffic.

"No, you are not going to my brother's club, Soph." Ava laughs.

"Why not? It's not my fault you were blessed with hot brothers," Sophia huffs.

"Because I said so. And, ew, don't talk about my brothers like that. I'm dropping you off at Hannah's and then I'm taking Dom home."

"Okay, first, Ava here was blessed with a hot cousin —her brothers are just okay. Second, drop me at Ash's. I'm crashing there," Dominic adds, and I look back to see the kid with his eyes closed and his head resting on the window.

"You're right. You are hot. But you're also a McKinley so you're out," Sophia says.

"Does Ash know you're going to his place?" Ava asks Dom, ignoring her friend's comment.

"Does Ash know you're hooking up with Noah Hunt?" Dominic sends back.

"Fine, I'll drop you at Ash's."

It took twenty minutes to get Ava alone. About fucking time. Those two idiots were getting on my last nerve.

"Okay, where to now?" She looks at me. She appears nervous and excited at the same time.

I punch the address into her state-of-the-art navigation system. Ava watches every detail. "Just follow the directions, babe."

"Rozelle Bay, what's there?" she asks as she side-eyes the GPS.

"It's a surprise—you'll see." I laugh at her frown.

"I don't like surprises, Noah. You know this about me already," she groans.

"You'll get used to them." I have put a lot of fucking thought into this night. I've been dreaming about it for over two years. I want this to be special for her. *Memorable.* I want her to be able to look back on her eighteenth birthday and know how much she is fucking loved. I want her to have no regrets about what we're going to do tonight. I fucking hope like fuck she likes what I've set up.

I can see that she's nervous, but she's not the only one. If ever there was a time in my life I didn't want to fuck things up, tonight is it. What if I hurt her? What if we go through with this and she doesn't feel the same way? Is she still too young? Should I be waiting longer?

We've talked about it. About us taking this step. She wanted to. Just two weeks ago. It was me who kept pushing for us to wait. Fuck, what if she sees everything set up and feels pressured to follow through?

I reach over and take hold of her hand. "Babe, you know there is absolutely no expectations tonight. This night is about you. I don't want you to do anything you're not ready for."

"Noah Hunt, if I wasn't one hundred percent ready, I wouldn't be here." The smile she sends my way eases some of my concerns.

We're at the dock within ten minutes. "Here, tap this on that post." I hand her the card to open the gates. We drive through and I direct her to the carpark closest to my private dock.

"Noah, if this is where you turn into a psychotic serial killer and feed me to the fishes, then you should probably know that I love you."

I'm stunned speechless. That's how she chooses to say those three words to me? I don't know how to respond to that. "Babe, if I were a psychotic serial killer, you would be the one person on earth I'd spare because I fucking love the shit out of you."

"Oh, okay. Well, what now?" she asks, looking through the windshield. It's the middle of the night. There's not much to see.

"Come with me." I take Ava's suitcase from the back of her car. I'm not sure why she packed so much. It's not like I'm planning on giving her a chance to wear clothes this weekend. At all.

I grab her palm with my free hand and lead her down the docks. My yacht, *Ava*, sits proudly at the far end. She's fucking beautiful, but nothing in comparison to her namesake. I bought this yacht a year ago. The first time I saw it, it's classical grace and beauty reminded me of the girl of my dreams. So like any sane man, I purchased her, came back the next day, and painted her new name across the side.

"Noah, are we going sailing?" Ava asks.

"Nah, not tonight. But we are staying on my boat," I say, stopping along the gangway.

Ava tilts her head upwards. The boat is lit up like a Christmas tree. "Ah, Noah, this is not a boat; it's a superyacht."

"It floats on water, travels on water. It's a boat, babe."

"Maybe to the rich and famous," she mumbles under her breath.

And I laugh. "A, you're driving around in a brand-new car that costs three-hundred and fifty-thousand dollars. You're hardly struggling, babe."

"The car was a birthday gift. What was I meant to do? Tell Josh: *thanks but no thanks*?"

"Joshua McKinley bought you that car?" I ask her, confused. Why the fuck would he buy her such an extravagant gift?

"Yep. Why?"

"I assumed your folks got it for you. Why would Josh buy you a car?"

"Because he likes to try to outdo my dad on gift-giving. They have a thing. Anyway, I'm not about to stop their competitive ways because I benefit in the long run."

"Huh. What did your dad give you?" If Josh gave her a car, what the fuck could top that?

"An apartment, near my dance school," she says.

"You're not living in an apartment alone, Ava." The words are out of my mouth before I can stop them.

13

You're not living in an apartment alone, Ava.

His words set off a blaze within me. I pull my hand out of his and storm ahead of him onto the deck of the boat—no, not *boat*, the bloody superyacht. Because of course Noah freaking Hunt wouldn't have a standard boat. No, he has to have the biggest and fanciest yacht in the marina.

I spin on my heel with my arms folded over my

chest. "You know what, Noah? Screw you. You don't get to dictate where or how I live. That's not how this is going to work."

I've been surrounded by arrogant, possessive cavemen my whole life. If I've learnt anything from my mum and aunts, it's that you have to stand your ground early on. Let them know exactly who's in charge of you. And newsflash: it's not him.

Noah smirks as his eyes rake up and down the length of my body. That cocky smirk only sends my rage to a whole new level.

"Argh, you are impossible." I stomp my way through the deck. The glass doors of the first-floor cabin slide open as I approach them. I only make it two steps inside before I pause. Tears form in the corners of my eyes at the scene laid out in front of me. There are pink hydrangeas everywhere, and petals make a path through the cabin. Candles of varying heights illuminate the intimate space, while pink and white balloons are artfully arranged around the room.

Noah's arms wrap around me from behind as my rage quickly dissipates. "Happy Birthday, babe," he whispers into my ear.

I let myself sink into his embrace. "You... you did all this for me? Noah, this is beautiful." I'm at a loss as to what to say.

"You deserve only the best, Ava. Come on, there's more to see."

With my hand enclosed in his and my eyes

attempting to take in every detail, we walk through the cabin, following the path of flower petals up the stairs. Noah leads us into a bedroom. And, again, my breath is stolen from my lungs with just how much effort he's put into tonight. This room is even more spectacular than the last. There are more candles, red roses everywhere, a champagne bucket with a bottle sitting on ice, and two glasses positioned on the table beside it.

Noah drops my hand, puts my suitcase down against the wall, and picks up a card that was placed next to the champagne glasses.

"Happy birthday, Ava." He passes me the card. And my hands tremble as I take it, sit on the edge of the bed, and open the envelope. As I lift the flap, a pink key drops onto my lap. I pick it up, slip the card free, and read the contents.

DEAR AVA,

I know it's your birthday, but every day since the night we met feels as though it's been mine. You are the greatest gift to ever come into my life, and I'll always cherish you like you deserve to be cherished.

The key is symbolic. You already own the key to my heart, my soul. And so I wanted to give you a key to my home, *our* home. We both know the penthouse doesn't have keys; however, I've had your fingerprint added to the elevator programming. You can now come and go as you please.

**Wishing you the happiest birthday today and for
years to come.**

Yours always,

Noah

BY THE TIME I finish reading, the tears are streaming
down my cheeks. I throw the card and key onto the bed
and jump up. Into his arms. He catches me, as he
always does.

"I love you. Thank you for doing all this—for
everything," I tell him right before I slam my lips onto
his. Our tongues dance, and there is nothing rushed
about this kiss. It's slow. We take our time exploring
each other. Loving each other.

Noah walks to the bed, gently laying us down in the
middle of the mattress. He hovers his body over mine,
bracing his weight on his elbows. "I have never loved
anything, anyone, as much as I love you, Ava." More
tears escape me. Noah catches them on his thumb. "We
don't have to, you know."

He's mistaking my reaction for sadness. "These are
happy tears, Noah. I want to. I want to give you this
part of me. I've never been more sure of anything."

He kisses me again, a little bit more urgently, as our
hands work to remove the layers of clothing separating
us. Noah sits me up to pull my dress over my head. I'm
wearing a matching white lace bra and panties.

"Fuck me, you're fucking gorgeous. Fucking mine."

Reaching around my back, he unclips my bra and slides the straps down my arms. His hands cup my breasts, pushing me back slightly so I fall onto the mattress. I thought I'd be more nervous in this moment. But the only thing running through my mind is whether I'm good enough for him. I sure hope so.

All thoughts disappear when his mouth latches on to one of my nipples. Noah has discovered how sensitive they are. He made me come just by playing with them the other night. "Oh God. Noah, I'm ready. I want to do this." I pull at his head until his face is above mine.

"You're sure?" he asks again.

"Very," I say. My panties are already soaked—evidence of how ready I am. Noah slides them down my legs. Then he stands and digs into his jeans pocket. Removing his briefs, he rips into the foil packet he's now holding between his teeth.

"You realise this makes you mine. There's no going back, Ava. This is us, forever. There is no one else. Ever," he says as he sheaths himself before settling between my legs.

"I will always be yours, Noah." I promise him everything, even though we're both more than aware that we have little control over our future.

"I'll go slow. Tell me if it's too much." He pushes the tip of his cock into my entrance. It feels strange. Tight. I'm almost afraid he's not going to fit when he drives in a little farther. "You good?" He doesn't take his eyes off mine.

"Uh-huh, don't stop," I tell him. It hurts, like a burning sensation, but I want this. I want to give him this. Noah pulls out. And then, without warning, he pushes back in. All the way. "Ahh." I feel like I've just been torn in half.

"Shit, babe. Are you okay?" His eyes glisten. Is he crying? I'm the one who's being ripped in two.

My hand reaches up to his cheek. "I'm fine. Just don't move for a minute."

He nods and brings his lips down to mine. We stay like that. Connected. With him buried inside me. Unmoving. After a few minutes, the burn starts to subside. I test it out, shifting my hips slightly. Noah groans and I still.

"Sorry," I whisper.

"Don't be. You just feel really fucking good, babe."

"Noah?"

"Yeah?"

"You can start moving now," I tell him. I watch as a look of relief washes over his face and he slowly starts to pull out of me to push back in. My legs wrap around his waist.

"I love you," he says as a tear drops onto my cheek.

"I love you—*oh God.*" A moan escapes my mouth as he hits some hidden place deep inside me. Noah reaches down and starts rubbing his fingers around my clit. God, that feels good. My whole body starts to tingle as I sense myself getting closer and closer to the edge.

"I want you to come for me, Ava. I need you to come with me," Noah grunts.

"Uh-huh." I can't form a proper response to anything right now. I can feel it—it's right there. I'm just about there.

"Now, Ava, fucking come for me." Noah swallows my screams as I fall over and plummet into the ecstasy below. His thrusts grow rigid, and then he stops moving. Buried inside me, he rests his head on my shoulder. "Fuck me," he pants. Then lifts his head. "Shit, are you okay, babe?" His eyes roam up and down my body as he quickly withdraws to sit upright.

I follow where his gaze landed. The spot between my legs. There's blood, but he doesn't look disgusted. He seems almost... proud?

"I'm sorry. I can..." What the hell can I do? I've just bled all over his white sheets, which probably cost more than my Jimmy Choos that are currently lying on the cabin floor.

"You don't have anything to be sorry for, Ava. This, what you've given me, I will always fucking treasure it. You are everything. I fucking love the absolute shit out of you, Ava. Don't ever doubt or forget it."

"I love you too." What else can I say to that speech?

"Come on, let's shower."

THE SUN SHINES straight onto my eyes as I blink them
open. Argh, it's too bright in here. Why is it so bright? I
roll over, hoping to escape the light, only to discover
this side's just as bright. Opening my eyes fully, I'm
greeted with a floor-to-ceiling window that's looking
out onto the ocean.

And the events of last night come back into focus.
Noah. The boat. What we shared. I stretch out my sore
limbs. I've had plenty of mornings where I've woken
up with sore, overworked muscles, but no number of
dance routines can equate to how used my body feels
right now.

I roll back over. The empty space on the mattress is
cold. I try to listen for movement, but I can't hear
anything. So I force myself from the bed, head for the
adjoining bathroom, freshen up, and put on the fluffy
pink robe that's hanging on the door. I try to retrace my
steps from last night. He has to be here somewhere.
This isn't just a regular boat, though; it's a bloody
floating mansion. He could be anywhere.

"Good morning, Miss Ava," a young girl in a blue
polo and a pair of khaki pants greets me.

"Ah, good morning," I reply.

"Mr Hunt is in the gym, but there is a full breakfast
buffet waiting in the dining room for you when you're
hungry."

"Thank you," I say, intent on finding Noah first.
"Ah, sorry... I didn't get your name?"

"It's Amy." She smiles.

"Thank you, Amy. Could you direct me to the gym?"

"Sure, follow me, Miss."

"You can just call me Ava," I tell her, and she nods her head.

I follow Amy through three different corridors before she points to a door. "Here you are. Just press the intercom on the wall in any of the rooms if you need anything." She disappears before I can thank her again.

Pushing the doors open, I find Noah at the weight bench. Damn, I wish I'd woken up earlier, because this is one show I'd watch for hours. I lean against the treadmill opposite him. Sweat drips down his body. He's only wearing a pair of shorts.

"Morning," he says, breaking me from my trance.

"Morning. Don't stop on my account." I smile as my eyes travel up and down those tanned abs, and I swear I can count eight. I've seen him naked plenty, but I've never stopped to fully appreciate each of those perfectly toned ridges. He has a freaking eight pack.

Noah smirks at me as he saunters over. He greets me with a panty-melting kiss. I say *panty-melting* because if I were actually wearing underwear, they'd be destroyed by now. "How'd you sleep?" he asks, pulling away.

"Better than I have in ages. You?"

"So good." He walks to a bench, picks up a bottle of

water, and downs half its contents in one go. How can drinking water look so bloody hot?

I shake my head and finally take in the rest of the room. I stop when my eyes find the wall of mirrors housing a barre and what looks like a five-foot, squared, timber dance floor. It's not a big space, but we're on a boat. "Do you often do barre exercises?" I ask Noah.

"No, but when I had the gym put in, I couldn't *not* add a spot for you," he answers.

"How long have you had this boat?"

"About a year." He wipes his torso with a towel.

A year? He's had this boat for a year... with a ballet area set aside just for me. I don't know how to feel about that. If I wasn't already a goner for this boy, I'd be running for the hills because he puts off crazy captor vibes to the max.

"Okay. What are your plans for today?" I ask him, choosing to ignore the last part.

"Ah, well, it's up to you. One of my mates is having a barbecue. They invited us to join if you want to go. Or we can hang out here all day."

"A barbecue? And they invited me?" I haven't met any of his friends yet. "It's not Brent, is it?" I don't think I want to go to a biker barbecue.

Noah laughs. "No, it's not Brent. It's one of my Army mates. There will be a whole heap of military guys and their wives. It's not a big deal. If you don't want to go, we don't have to."

"Do you want me to meet your friends? I mean, I get it if you don't want that yet." I don't really, but I can pretend.

"Ava, I'm more than prepared to put an ad up on the biggest billboard in Sydney. Fuck, I'll even throw in a signwriter to make sure no one mistakes my claim on you. Of course I want you to meet my friends. Why the fuck wouldn't I?"

"Well, I don't know. Because I'm so much younger than you?"

"Two years is hardly a big age gap, babe."

"Okay, so I guess we're going to a barbecue. Shit, how long do I have to get ready?" I start to panic. I need to make a good first impression.

"Ah, we can leave in an hour. You don't need to get all dolled up, though, babe. You look fucking perfect as you are right now."

I peek at my reflection in the mirror and cringe. "I have bed hair and I'm wearing a robe. I look like shit, Noah."

"You look like you've been thoroughly fucked. I like it." He wraps his arms around me, and my head falls to his still-damp chest.

I pause for a moment before pushing him away. "Sorry, I gotta rush. I don't have long to get ready." I can hear Noah's laughter follow me down the hall as I try to find my way back to the main cabin.

14

I take a cup of orange juice and a muffin up to the room. The room that now looks like it's been ransacked. There are clothes and shoes everywhere. How the fuck did she even fit all this in that one suitcase? No wonder the thing was fucking heavy.

"Ava, babe, you still alive in here?" I call out.

"Over here." Her voice comes from the bathroom.

Standing at the door, I let my eyes roam to her feet

—now covered in a pair of black Louboutins—and travel up her long, lean legs to the hem of her Louis Vuitton dress.

"I won't be much longer."

My gaze meets hers in the mirror. Her hands are busy twisting strands of her hair around a curling iron. Her face is impeccably made up. Dark eyes with those fucking bright-red lips I want wrapped around my cock.

Fuck. "Ah, babe, you know it's just a backyard barbecue, right?" I ask her.

"Yeah." She nods, her fingertips focused on the task at hand.

Shit, these guys don't know I'm from money. How the fuck do I tell her she needs to tone down the *I'm a rich girl* thing she has going on? Don't get me wrong, she looks fucking hot as hell. But her outfit screams wealth.

"The guys don't know who I am, Ava," I tell her, putting the orange juice and muffin on the counter that's now covered in her supplies. Doing my best to ignore the mess and my need to fucking clean it up, I lean against the basin's edge and peer down at her.

"What do you mean they don't know who you are? I thought you said they were friends."

"They are. They don't know about my family, though. And all this." I point around the opulent bathroom. "They don't know I come from money."

"Why?" she asks, her eyebrows drawn down.

"Because it's different in the Army. Nobody judges me or tries to get shit out of me. I like being one of the guys, you know." I shrug. I don't know how else to explain it.

"Okay, I won't let the cat out of the bag that you're richer than Richie Rich." She peeks down at her dress. "I'll change. I have some more casual options," she says.

As it turns out, her *casual option* consists of a pair of Gucci denim shorts that are way too fucking short, white converse high-tops, and a white blouse that's so sheer I recognize the pink lacey bra she's sporting beneath it.

"What? Too casual?"

"Too much fucking skin showing is more like it," I growl.

"Oh well, yeah, you'll get used to that." She smiles, walking towards me.

"Ah, babe?" I ask.

"Yeah?"

"Any chance you want to leave that Chanel bag behind?"

She looks from me to the bag. "You know, we could always let them think I'm like your sugar mumma or something?" she suggests.

～

"Are you sure I look okay?" Ava is nervously fidgeting with her top as we walk up the footpath to my mate Hugo's house.

"Babe, you'd look fucking hot in a paper bag. Besides, I don't give a fuck what anyone thinks of you, and you shouldn't care either."

"Thanks," she murmurs.

I set down the cooler bag holding a six pack of beer and knock on the door.

"Come in," a voice hollers from inside the house.

"What? No doorman or waitstaff? I can't believe you can rough it with us little people," Ava whispers in mock disbelief.

I roll my eyes. "Shut up. You're as much of a spoilt trust fund baby as I am," I whisper back to her.

"Hardly. I may have a trust fund but I guarantee you it doesn't have the same number of zeros at the end."

"You haven't seen the trust fund I had set up for you this week." I smirk at her shocked expression.

"What?"

"We can talk about this later." I pull her through the house and out the back, where a heap of my mates are already lounging on the deck.

"He's alive. Where the fuck you been, Hunt?" Jimbo calls out.

"Fuck off." I shake his hand. "This is my girl—Ava." Pointing to each of the guys, I say, "Ava, that's Jimbo, Ted, Kyle, and Hugo."

"Hi. Ah, you have a lovely home, Hugo," she offers shyly. It's a different crowd from what she's used to.

"Ah, thanks?" Hugo replies with drawn-down eyebrows.

"So, Ava, how'd a nice girl like you get mixed up with Hunt here?"

"Um, well, he saved me from a flat tyre and the rest is history," she answers, smiling up at me.

"Have a seat. Burgers are just about done. Natasha's inside finishing off the salads." Hugo points to an empty deck chair.

I pull Ava towards it, sit down, and tug at her arm until she falls onto my lap. It doesn't take her long to relax against my chest. I grab a beer out of the cooler and offer it to her. She shakes her head, so I put it down. We sit there, shooting the shit with my mates and their girls. Ava fits in effortlessly. I have no idea what she was so worried about. She's a fucking natural at social gatherings.

"So, what do you do, Ava?" Natasha, Hugo's wife, asks over lunch.

"She's a dancer," I answer for her. I can't help the smile that breaks out on my face. I'm so fucking proud of her. Ted and Kyle both choke on their food. "Get you're fucking thoughts out of the gutter, assholes. She's a fucking ballerina." I glare at them, knowing exactly what kind of dancer they were picturing.

Ava takes hold of my hand under the table, rubbing her thumb in small soothing circles.

"Holy shit, no way. A ballerina? I've never met a ballerina before," Hugo says.

"Well, we're a rare breed, I guess," Ava answers.

"I like this one. You know, if you wake up one day and come to your senses about your choice in guys, I'll be around," Ted, the only fucking single one here, says. The fucker is looking for a fight.

"I doubt that's ever going to happen, so you probably shouldn't hold your breath," Ava replies casually. Meanwhile, I'm fucking fuming. If looks could kill, he'd be fucking dead right now.

"So, when do you start the big camp?" Hugo asks, changing the subject. Fuck, I was really hoping this wouldn't come up.

"No date yet." I shrug.

"What's the big camp?" Ava turns to me.

"It's nothing," I say at the same time fucking Ted opens his big mouth with, "Your boy's upping his training. Three months of camp and he'll be one of the top dogs."

"Oh, okay." She drops it, but I see the questions in her eyes. The sorts of questions I know she's not about to ask here.

Ava is quiet on the way back to the marina. "What's wrong?" I ask, taking hold of her hand, only to have her pull it back.

"What exactly is this big camp? And what are you training for?" she responds.

"I can't tell you, Ava. It's classified," I say honestly.

"It's classified? Why is it classified?"

"Because it's the fucking Defence Force, babe. Everything's classified."

"Okay, well, where is this big camp? Do you have to go away? How long will you be gone? Surely you can tell me that."

"It's three months of seven days a week training. If I make it through, I have no idea where they'll send me after that."

"What-what does this mean for us?" she stutters.

"Ava, nothing is changing for us. You are mine. No matter how long I have to go away, I'll always come back for you. Always."

"And I'm meant to be okay with this? With you going off and doing God knows what? Just sit here, twiddle my thumbs, and wait for you to come home?"

"No, you'll be chasing your dreams, Ava. You'll be dancing. You'll be so busy you'll hardly notice I'm gone."

"Doubtful."

"I'm sorry," I tell her, because I fucking hate seeing her this upset.

It's not until we're lying in bed later that night, her head resting on my chest, that I tell her the truth. "I'm training for the SAS," I whisper into the darkness. Ava's body tenses up. Shit, I fucking thought for sure she was asleep.

Before I know it, she's sitting upright. "No!" she says.

"Fuck, babe, I thought you were sleeping. Forget you heard that," I plead with her.

"No! You can't."

"What do you mean no?" I reach out for her but she's quick to jump off the bed. I watch as she paces the room like a caged animal.

"You can't do this to me, Noah. No. You have to tell them you've changed your mind. Quit. You don't even need to work that job. Why the bloody hell would you sign up for the most dangerous assignment of them all?"

"Babe, I can't quit. This is my job. Also, people don't just quit the Defence Force, A. It's a long process to get out," I attempt to explain. Ava stops pacing and falls to the ground. I cautiously walk over and sit down in front of her. "Please, A, I need this..." I wipe the tears from her cheeks. "I'm sorry. Please don't cry"

"I don't want to lose you. People who go to war *die*, Noah," she cries.

"I'm not going to die." And just like that, the promise we both know I can't keep falls from my lips. "Besides, it'll be years before I'm even sent anywhere." It won't be, but I figure it'll buy me the time I need for her to get used to the idea of dating a soldier.

"Really? Years?"

"Probably."

"When do you leave for training?"

"Four weeks."

"Okay, well, let's make the most of the next four weeks then. I can cut back on rehearsals, and we can spend more time together. I need more time."

"You're not cutting back on your rehearsals. You're not giving up something you love doing for me, babe."

"But I love you more," she says.

"I know, but dancing is part of you. You're not cutting back. I'll drag my arse out of bed every morning to watch you rehearse. Watching you dance is not a hardship." I smirk.

"Noah, wherever you are, wherever they send you, please always come back for me."

"I will always come back to you, A. You're my future —my everything." I pick her up and carry her to the bed.

15

Six months later

My feet are aching and my legs feel like they're going to detach from my body, but I continue pushing myself. Tonight is the last show for two weeks.

I can't wait to have lazy sleep-ins. Endless Netflix-and-chill sessions with Noah. I promised I'd spend the entire second week of break at his place. Right after New Year's Eve. He's been bugging me to introduce him to my family. To stop sneaking around with him. I finally caved and invited him to Christmas Eve dinner at my aunt's. The only problem is... I haven't actually told my family he's coming yet. I'm hoping that once he's there and they see how much we love each other, my dad and uncles won't be able to scare him away. Or kill him.

Noah's promised that nothing will ever scare him away from me. We may have been dating for only six months, but I feel like I've known him my whole life. This love we share, it's like nothing I've ever felt. Even when he's gone for weeks at a time with work, which happens often, he always comes back. He completed his three months of training. I haven't asked much about it, though I know I'm not meant to know anything at all.

When he finally came back home after those three months, he told me he was going to get out. I cried more tears of relief that night than I ever have in my life. We've planned out our whole future together, starting with the new year when he's a free man. I'm not sure what changed his mind. After my birthday weekend and the initial shock, I never again brought up the fact that I wanted him to quit. I realised how selfish it was of me to expect that from him. I fell in love with Noah, and that includes all the parts of him.

I can feel him in the audience tonight, though he's

not meant to be here. We arranged to meet tomorrow afternoon when I'd bring him home to meet my family. The curtains finally close and I lean over with my hands on my hips, attempting to catch my breath. I know my brother Ash is waiting for me. He's driving me up to my aunt's beach house tonight.

Exiting the stage door, I smile as I see Noah leaning against the wall. As I walk towards him, I notice he isn't returning the smile. In fact, he looks... sad. Nervous. Then it hits me. He's wearing his uniform.

I shake my head, the tears already streaming down my face. I fling my arms around his neck. Maybe if I hold on tight enough, he won't be able to leave.

"I'm so sorry, babe. I'm so fucking sorry," he whispers into my ear. I take a step back.

"No, you're not leaving. Tell me you're not. You can't," I cry. Noah is stoic; he doesn't move an inch. I hear my older brother calling out my name, but I choose to ignore him. My hands push at Noah's chest before they start pounding against him.

"I'm sorry, A. I don't have a choice. I have to." His voice is quiet.

"Ava, what the fuck is going on here?" My brother growls as he comes up next to me.

"Ash, nothing is going on. Noah was just leaving." I turn towards the exit, my heart shattering piece by piece with every centimetre that separates us.

"I'm sorry, A. I really am. If I could change this, I would." Noah attempts to reach out for me, and I step back again, unable to stop the tears from free-falling. Ash wraps his arms around me, forever the protective big brother.

"Can you make sure she doesn't open this until Christmas Day? Please. Look after her for me."

I can only assume Noah is talking to Ash. I can't look at him. I can't watch him walk away. I can't watch the future I dreamt of disappear. So, I do the only thing I can do. I bury my head into my brother's chest and take comfort in his arms, which are currently the only thing holding me upright.

"A, I will come back to you. I promise," Noah says. That has me lifting my head.

"You can't promise that, Noah. You can't *know* that," I yell to his retreating back.

"Ava, what the fuck? You better start talking before I go kick the ass of one of our soldiers. I'd really fucking hate to do that. But for you, I will," Ash growls.

"No, you won't. Don't worry about it. Whatever it was, it's gone now. He's leaving. I'm fine. Let's go. I'm ready to hit the beach." I wipe my wet cheeks, take out my compact from my purse, and fix my makeup as I walk outside to Ash's car.

I thought I'd be able to use the ride to the beach house to clear my mind. To sit in silence and prepare the mask I'm going to have to wear for the next few days, so everyone doesn't know that my soul is slowly dying.

"Ava, honey, you know you can come and talk to me

about anything. I'll always be here for you." Ash's voice is calm, but his knuckles are white as he grips the steering wheel.

"I know," I tell him. Because I do know that, but this isn't something I want to talk to anyone about.

"So, Noah... Who is he, and how do we know him?" he asks.

"You don't know him. I don't even know him. Not anymore. I thought I could talk him out of joining. I thought I would be important enough for him to stay. Guess I was wrong."

"How long have you known him, Ava?" And here comes the interrogation I've been avoiding for the last six months.

"We went to school together. He was two years above me. I've known him since I was thirteen, Ash. But in the last few months, we started dating. I just didn't... I don't know. I didn't expect he'd actually do it."

"Do what?" he asks.

"Sign up. He was meant to be leaving the job, getting out. He promised he was getting out. I know a lot of his friends signed up for a tour overseas somewhere. But he said he was getting out." I sound like a broken record.

"It's a noble job, Ava. Also, what the fuck? Why didn't I know you were dating? Do Mum and Dad know?"

"Ah, no, they do not, and you're not going to tell

them. Besides, it doesn't matter. He's gone now." Well, technically, my mum knows something but Ash doesn't need to know that. It will only cause drama if he mentions it to my dad first.

"Yeah, well, it kind of sounded like he had plans of coming back. Where are they sending him anyway?"

"He's... I'm not meant to say anything. I'm not even meant to know."

"Sweetheart, you know whatever you tell me will never leave this car. You need to talk to someone, otherwise it's going to eat you up inside, and you'll end up a crazy old cat lady."

"A crazy cat lady sounds good. At least her heart would be safe from being broken." Maybe I'll ask Dad to buy me a kitten for Christmas.

"Is your heart broken, Ava?"

"Right now, it feels like it's beyond repair. How can he just leave like that?" I ask him.

"I don't know, honey." He reaches over and squeezes my hand. "I do know that if you're in the military, you don't really have a choice where they send you."

He's defending him? What the hell?

"But that's just it. He didn't have to go and apply for the bloody special forces. But no, not Noah fucking Hunt. He has to be the best of the best. Always." I hate and love that about him.

"Ava, you really can't tell anyone. You could get him in a lot of trouble for knowing that he's special forces, or going to be." My brother looks at me like he wants to lock me away in a tower somewhere and never let me out. How do I know? Because my dad looks at me the same way.

"I know. But I hate him so much right now... Maybe you should go kick his ass for me, Ash." I smile at him. I wish I could take comfort in the idea, but even that's not the least bit appealing.

"I'd love to, sweetheart. Maybe after the Christmas break. I'll track him down for you and do just that."

"Thanks, Ash, you know you're my favourite brother today," I tell him.

"Anytime, sweetheart."

I spend the rest of the drive staring out the window, urging myself not to cry. Trying not to replay every moment Noah and I shared over the last six months. This Christmas is going to be the worst.

Ash stops out front of Aunt Ella's house. "I might just drop you and run. I need to check into my rental real quick before I come back here."

"Okay, sure." I smile, lean over, and kiss him on the cheek. "Thank you for being my brother, Ash."

"Wouldn't have it any other way, sweetheart."

16

Noah

I've never hated myself more than I do right now. The image of Ava's face streaked with tears will haunt me for the rest of my life. I did that to her. I promised her I was getting out, and what the fuck did I go and do? I fucking pulled my transfer request at the last minute to get deployed with my mates. I can't *not* go with them. What kind of fucking soldier lets his mates go off alone, while he stays home living a life full of fucking luxuries they'll never experience?

I have to believe she'll wait for me. I have to keep faith that when I return, we'll move on with our lives. Pick up right where we left off. It's like I've pressed the pause button. When I get home, I'll make it up to her. I have to believe that she'll let me.

I'm sitting here on this plane surrounded by mates —all with similar looks on their faces—trying to hide the pain of leaving loved ones behind. The uncertainty that we might not actually make it back thickening the air. What the fuck have I done?

This was meant to be the weekend I met her family, the weekend we stopped sneaking around. Now, it's locked in our history as the weekend I broke her fucking heart and walked away. At least she's not alone. She has her family. They won't let her break. They'll help her.

Fuck! She was the only good fucking thing I've ever had, and I just fucking left her. I go to pull my phone from my pocket. I want to call her, text her. But I can't. Because I don't fucking have a phone. We were stripped of all our personal devices before we boarded the flight.

It's not for long. I have to keep telling myself that. I'll be home before we know it. She'll hardly notice that I'm gone. This mission is meant to be four weeks—*tops.* That's the plan. Four weeks and we can continue like I never left.

What's four weeks when we have the rest of our lives together?

Nothing. I close my eyes and lean my head back. It will be okay. It has to be.

WE LANDED ON CHRISTMAS DAY. It took two fucking days and three different flights before we reached our destination. A fucking camp in the centre of the goddamn middle eastern desert. I thought I knew what hot was—Australia has cruel fucking summers—but this heat, it's unlike anything I've ever experienced. The fucking dirt, the dust.

There're six of us, all selected for this particular assignment. I look at the five men I would take a bullet for and thank my fucking lucky stars I have them covering my ass out here. We're going over the mission plan. It's a simple extraction. Get in, grab the target, and get out. We have four weeks to make it happen. Intel is spread out across the table. Picture after picture. Looking over the details, I'm thinking we'll be home before we know it.

"Just like stealing candy from a fucking baby." Hugo smirks.

"Don't get cocky, son. That's what'll get you and them killed out there." CO Jackson points to each one of us.

"Sorry, sir." Hugo salutes.

"Right, moving on. You all have three weeks to memorise everything in this packet. Then we move out."

I reach forward and take the documents from my superior's hands. Three fucking weeks of sitting around this shithole before we can converge and get the fucking job done.

"Dismissed," the CO says.

All six of us stand to attention, salute, and exit the tent.

"I gotta make a call. Catch you guys later." I tuck the yellow envelope under my arm and make my way to the comms tent. I should call her—Ava. I fucking need to hear her voice. See if she opened my gift. Ask if she's holding up okay. I don't though. Instead, I put a call through to Brent. It almost rings out by the time he answers.

"Yep," he says in greeting.

"Took you fucking long enough," I reply.

"Noah? It's the fucking middle of the night. What the fuck do you want?"

"I need you to check in on Ava for me. Go to my apartment. There's an envelope in the safe with her name on it. I need you to give it to her."

"Why can't you do it?"

"Because I can't. I'm not home. Just do it, Brent. You know the code to the safe."

"Where the fuck are you? And what's with the sirens? If you're over in some stupid fucking country tryin' to get your arse killed, Hunt, I'll fucking save everyone the effort and shoot you myself."

"Well, let's hope you get the chance. Just give her the envelope and tell her I'm sorry. Tell her... Just give her the envelope." I hang up the satellite phone.

I can't call her. If she hears the fucking constant sirens, sounds of explosions and gunshots that are fucking 24/7 background noise here, she'll worry more than she should. So I do the next best thing, I pull out a piece of paper and a pen and write her a letter. I'll probably be home before she even gets it, but I write it anyway.

DEAR AVA,

I know it's not conventional (and cliché as fuck) to be writing you letters from afar. But that's exactly what I plan to do until the day arrives that I can come home to you. I also know that you can't write back, and I know you probably hate me right now after the way things ended. But I don't care. I love you. I will always love you, Ava. It's always been you. Did I ever tell you about the first time I saw you?

You were wearing a yellow leotard. I think you were meant to be a lion or a lioness. You were dancing in the school's *The Lion King* production. You were the star. Of course you were. You have this uncanny ability to shine so bright that it blinds everything else around you.

I remember sitting in the back row of the auditorium with my mates. They were all joking around and being rowdy, and then you came on stage. And everything else faded into the background. You see —that moment—the first time I saw you, you didn't see me. But when you looked out at the audience, I could have sworn the smile you wore was meant just for me.

This was four years ago. You were only in the tenth grade while I was in twelfth. You were so young, but I knew it then. That you were mine. You will always be mine, Ava.

For the next few years, I watched you. I wanted you. I will never stop wanting you. It took two years for fate to intervene and finally bring us together. Two years I waited for you to notice me back, to want me back. But it was worth it. Because that first kiss, that first touch, those moments will be forever burned on my soul.

I wish I could tell you about where I am, what I'm doing here. But I can't. What I can tell you is that I'm sorry. I'm sorry I made you feel like you don't matter, because you do. I'm sorry I made you feel like I left you. Because I haven't. I haven't left, Ava. I'm still with you. I'm still there with you. Every time I close my eyes, I see you.

It's hard here, harder than I thought. Would I rather be snuggled up in bed with you? Fuck yes. But

I made a commitment, and despite being away from you, I love this job.

Did you get the necklace? I have an image in my head. An image of you wearing it, of that little slipper sitting between your breasts.

I've got to go. But I'll write again soon. I promise.

Yours always,

N

17

It's Christmas Day. This Christmas has been like no other. Lily went and caught the attention of Aunt Ella's new neighbour, Alex. I'm pretty certain he's in the mafia or something just as dangerous. I guess that probably doesn't matter much to Lily. I can see in her eyes how quickly she's fallen for this guy. What shocks me the most is how accepting Uncle Bray is about the whole thing.

I wonder if my dad would have accepted Noah that easily. Somehow I doubt it. Ash keeps glancing at me. He hasn't mentioned Noah but he's been checking up on me. Like right now, we're sitting around after everyone has opened their gifts and he's staring at me.

"Ava, come outside with me for a sec," he says, walking out of the room. I follow him because frankly, whatever he has to say, I'd rather he say it away from everyone else. We stop at his car. I wait as he opens the boot and pulls out a gift box. A small gift box. The small gift box Noah gave him.

"No, I don't want it, Ash. Throw it out." I shake my head, making no move to take the gift.

"Ava, trust me, you want to open this, sweetheart. If you don't, you're going to regret it, always wonder *what if.*"

Why is he doing this to me? He's meant to be the one scaring boys away, not encouraging me to open something from the one who just broke my heart. "If Noah wanted to give me a Christmas gift, he should have been here to give it to me himself." I fold my arms over my chest.

"Ava, the kid might be entering into the special forces, but he wouldn't have survived ten minutes here trying to be your boyfriend." Ash smirks.

"Ash, I can't open it." I can't. Why can't this day be over? I want to go home, curl up in bed, and sleep for the rest of my life. Probably with a dozen cats nestled around me to keep me company.

"Yes, you can. Here, I'll stay with you."

I finally take the gift box and remove the lid. There's a letter and a small jewellery box inside. I grab the letter and put it in my pocket. I then remove the little tiffany-blue box, letting the outer packaging drop to the ground. I can't help the tears that form in the corners of my eyes as I pull out a rose gold chain with a matching ballet slipper dangling from the centre. The chain twists in the breeze and the words *'never stop dancing'* appear on the underside of the pendant.

I almost collapse to the ground when Ash catches me, pulling me into his chest. His arms wrap around me so tight it's like he's attempting to hold my soul together. Except he can't. It's already destroyed.

"It's going to be all right, Ava. I know you don't believe that now, but you're young and you have your whole life ahead of you," Ash whispers into my hair as he kisses the top of my head.

I pull away from him. "I'm going to buy a cat. If this is what love feels like, then I don't want anything to do with it." I wipe at my face before spinning and holding the chain around the back of my neck. "Help me do this up, please."

"Ava, tell me what I can do to fix this for you. I'll do anything." It's as if my brother can somehow feel my pain. As if he's about to break down and cry with me.

For me.

"Nothing. There's nothing anyone can do. Just don't tell anyone, please, Ash," I plead.

"I promise I won't tell a soul, sweetheart. Come on, let's get in there and get this whole Christmas thing over with." He drapes an arm over my shoulder and leads me back into the house.

"Yeah. We still have to make it through Boxing Day at the McKinley Ranch," I remind him. Every Boxing Day, we all get up at the crack of dawn and fly down to the McKinleys' ranch in the Hunter Valley. Ash has made so many excuses over the past few years to avoid going there. But considering he's now dating Breanna McKinley, something tells me he'll be making an appearance this time around.

THREE HOURS LATER, I ride home with my parents and Axe—who thankfully doesn't shut up the whole way there. I know he's doing it to take attention off me. If the fact that he keeps looking over at me with questioning eyes didn't give that away, it's obvious when he reaches over and grabs hold of my hand, squeezing it slightly before letting it go.

"Finally. I thought we'd never make it here," Axe says as we pull into the driveway.

"You almost didn't. I was ready to throw your arse out fifty kilometres back," Dad grunts. Then he looks at my mum. "Surely there's a pill or something to fix that," he suggests, pointing back at my brother.

"Leave him alone. He's just excited. It's Christmas, Zac," Mum says.

"You know I can hear you guys, right?" Axe huffs while exiting the car.

"Yep, just like we could hear you the whole way home." Mum smirks at him.

"All right, I'm tired. Catch you guys later." I make a quick escape up to my bedroom and shut the door. And I'm only on my bed for five minutes before there's a knock.

"Ava, sweetheart, can I come in?" Dad calls out as he opens the door and walks inside without waiting for a response.

"Sure, Dad, help yourself."

"Don't mind if I do." He places a cup of hot chocolate on my bedside table. "Thought you might need this."

"Thanks." I try my hardest not to cry. I can hold it together for just a little while longer. I know I can.

"Fuck. I knew something was wrong. What the fuck happened, Ava?" My dad sits down on my bed and scoops me up against his side.

"Nothing," I say into his shoulder.

"It's clearly not *nothing*. What's made you cry? Or who?"

"He wasn't supposed to leave me. Why'd he have to leave me, Dad?" I choke on a sob.

"Honey, I have no idea who you're talking about? Who left?" He kisses the top of my head as his fingers run through my hair, attempting to soothe my pounding heartbeat.

"Noah, he wasn't meant to leave. I need him," I cry harder.

"Ava, Noah who? You really need to catch me up here."

I sit upright and lean my back against the bed. "Noah Hunt... I've been dating him for six months."

"Six... what? You've been dating?" My dad looks like he wants to throw up. "How the fuck did I not know about this? When? How?"

"I..." I don't know what to say through my tears.

"Sweetheart, it's okay. And let me tell you, you are Ava Williamson. Strong, beautiful Ava Williamson. You don't need anybody, you hear me. You have me. You have your mum. You will always have us."

"I... I love him, and he left." I can't seem to push past my grief to hear anything my dad is saying.

"I'm going to fucking kill him." He pulls out his phone.

"What? No, stop! You can't. Besides, he's probably not even in the country now. They sent him somewhere."

"Who sent him where?"

"The Army. He got deployed," I explain.

"Ava, you've been dating a fucking soldier? How fucking old is this guy?" My dad jumps to his feet and starts pacing the room—yep, he's losing his shit.

"Relax. He's only two years older than me," I tell him. Which does not relax him at all.

My dad continues to march back and forth, wearing a path into my hardwood floors. "Did he hurt you? Did he force you to do something you didn't want to do?"

"What? No, of course not. He just tore my heart out and stomped all over it. But, no, Noah would never hurt me on purpose." As I say the words, I know they're true. "This is why I didn't tell you. I knew you'd freak out like you are now."

That has my father stopping in his tracks. "Ava, sweetheart, I'm sorry. You're my little girl. I'm not ready for you not to be. Tell me how I can fix this for you."

What is it with all the men in my life asking that? They can't fix it. They can't bring Noah home. They can't turn back time to make it so that he never left in the first place.

"I just want to sleep. I need to sleep," I tell him.

"Okay. I'll be downstairs if you need anything else," he says.

I close my eyes and take deep breaths. But the problem with closing my eyes is that I see his face. His smile. His eyes. If I focus hard enough, I can even smell him.

My door creaks open, and I don't even bother looking this time. Maybe if I pretend I'm asleep, whoever it is will go away.

"Ava, I know you're awake. Sit up." It's my mum's

no-nonsense voice. Shit. I push upright as she kicks the door closed behind her. She's holding two tubs of mint chocolate ice cream and a couple of spoons. "I know it's cliché, but we're doing this. Come on, it'll make you feel better, baby."

"Dad told you?" I ask, not the least bit surprised.

"Your father is downstairs cursing and losing his mind because he just found out his little girl is all grown up." My mum smirks. "So, Noah Hunt, huh? Not bad."

"What? How do you know him?"

"His mother and I cross paths at events." She shrugs. "Also, he's a Hunt—that family is in the papers more than Josh and Emmy," she says, referring to the McKinleys.

"They are. But Noah stays out of the public eye."

"So how'd you meet him?" Mum asks as she sits next to me. She hands over one of the tubs with a spoon. I take the offering. It's not going to make me feel any better though.

"I had a flat tyre. He gave me a lift home." I shrug. That memory feels like it was so long ago.

"Why didn't you bring him around yet? How could you possibly date someone and keep it a secret from this family for so long? It's actually impressive." She laughs.

"Axe and Dom know."

"Huh, you must have some powerful dirt on those two for them not to give that info up." She smiles. I've often wondered why Axe never said anything. I know Dom probably forgot all about it after that night at the club. "Were you safe, Ava?" Mum asks.

"Yes," I say, though I'm immediately reminded of that one time a few weeks ago when we weren't so safe. I'd turned up at Noah's apartment after dance, making sure I wasn't wearing any panties. My skirt was on the shorter side of short, and my black blouse was practically see-through.

"Noah, you here?" I call out.

"In here, babe." Noah's voice comes from down the hall. I find him in the games room. He's shooting balls around the pool table by himself.

"Hi." I wrap my arms around him and claim his mouth.

"Mmm, I missed you," he says, sucking on my neck.

"Not as much as I missed you. I'll play you. Winner gets to choose the movie tonight," I reply, plucking the pool cue from his hand.

"Deal. You can be smalls."

I look over my shoulder at him as I bend at the waist, lining the cue up with the white ball. I see the moment his eyes drift to my ass— and they widen.

"What the fuck, A? Where the fuck are your panties?" he growls.

I hit the ball, totally miss the shot I was aiming for, and straighten up. I don the most innocent look I can muster. "Oh, I must have forgotten them." I bite into my bottom lip for good measure.

"You forgot them?" He stalks towards me, plucks the cue

out of my hand, and throws it aside. His palms fall to my waist as he lifts me onto the table. "You know what happens to good girls who do bad things? Like forget to wear their panties, A?" he asks.

"No, what happens?" I spread my legs wide, and my skirt hitches up higher as Noah steps between my open thighs.

"They get their greedy little pussy filled. They get fucked. Is that what you want, A? You want me to fill that hungry little pussy up? Fuck it like only I can?"

I nod my head. "Yes, let's do that." I'm eager to do just that.

Noah unfastens his jeans. He has his cock out within seconds and is pushing it into me.

"Oh God, yes." I scream. He feels so good. Why does it feel this good? It's different. Maybe it's the urgency of his thrusts.

"Fuck, you feel good, baby. You like that? You like getting fucked hard and fast?" he grunts.

"Yes, oh God, Noah," I cry out as he relentlessly pounds into me. He grabs my legs and bends them back over my shoulders, the position allowing him to go even deeper. I don't know what spot he's hitting inside me, but damn, I'm about to explode.

"Fuck, I love your tight little pussy. It's mine, A. All. Fucking. Mine," Noah grits out between clenched teeth.

We both scream as the orgasm rolls over each of us, like a wave that just doesn't stop. It keeps going and going.

Eventually, Noah lowers my legs and pulls out of me. And I swear I hear my core whimper at the sudden loss.

"Fuck, shit. I'm sorry." He curses as he looks down between my thighs.

"What? What happened?"

"I didn't use a condom. I'm so sorry, A."

"We didn't. It was both of us. It's fine. It'll be okay. I take the pill every day, Noah. Religiously."

"Ava, want to tell me about him?" my mum says, drawing me from my thoughts.

"He's the beginning and end of my entire world. And now he's gone, so where does that leave me?"

"Oh, honey. It's going to be okay. I promise." She tugs me to her side. I really wish everyone would stop making promises they can't keep.

18

The days are long out in the desert; the nights are even longer. And sleep? Yeah, that's a fucking fantasy at this point. The constant sounds of war surround me. I've been through what they claim is the toughest of the toughest training. But nothing can really prepare you for the reality of a warzone.

We went on a recon mission last night, making our

way into the city. I've never been more fucking thankful to be an Australian than when I saw what was happening beyond the walls of the camp. The devastation. Burnt-down buildings. Children begging in the streets. Little boys walking around with AK-47s instead of backpacks. These kids should be in school, not being used as fucking cannon fodder.

Our objective point is the most heavily guarded building in the city. Not enough to keep us out though. They won't even see us coming. I wanted to just storm the place last night, get to the target, and get the fuck home. It's only been a few days, and I knew I'd miss her. But, fuck, I didn't expect this ache in my chest.

Sure, I've done trips away a few times, but I was always in the same fucking country. Not on the other side of the world. It fucking physically hurts. I fucking hate it. I haven't called Brent back yet to see if she got the package. Or to ask about her reaction.

I close my eyes and picture her dancing. It's like I have all of her routines on a video loop. Memorised. She has two weeks off from the dance company, but I know her. She'll be there right now, rehearsing her audition piece for The Australian Ballet Company. I have no doubt she'll get the position she's going for. She was born to be up on that stage.

I pull out the notepad and paper.

DEAR AVA,

The days are so fucking long. Your face, knowing that I have you to come home to, that's what gets me through.

At least I fucking hope I have you to come home to. I know you're pissed at me, babe, but this trip isn't going to last long. I'll probably be home before you even read these letters.

Do you remember the spot I took you to, on that first night? You asked me what I saw when I looked out into the darkness. I told you I saw peace. What I should have told you... What I was too afraid to tell you at the time was that I saw you. When I look out into the nothingness so full of potential, I can see you. I see you dancing. I see you smiling. Laughing. I see you in a white dress. I see you as a mother to our children. I see our future.

Peace. You are my peace. A, you are everything that matters to me. I know you probably can't believe that right now, because I'm not there. But it's the truth. I fucking love you. In this life and the next.

Don't give up on us, A. We will have our future.

Always yours,

Noah

I FOLD the paper in half and place it in an envelope. I write her name on the front. I really fucking hope she gets these letters, but mostly I hope I'm home before she reads them. I'd like to tell her these things in person. I should have told her all of this before I left.

"Beer?" Hugo walks into the tent and sits on his cot, leaning his rifle up against his thigh. Keeping it close. Never far away. Have you ever had to sleep fully clothed with boots on and a loaded fucking rifle in your grip? It's not fucking comfortable.

"Sure." I take the offered beer.

"Writing poetry?" He nods to the envelope.

"Writing my truths. To Ava."

"How's she doing? It's always the hardest the first time. It'll get easier for her," he says.

"Yeah," I agree, knowing there'll never be a next time. "How do you do it? You have a wife and a kid on the way. How do you just leave them behind?"

Hugo observes me silently for a while, without answering. "Those kids you saw out there today, they're someone's kids. Wives, daughters, sons are all being killed out there every fucking day. We're not just here to neutralise a target, Hunt. We're here to save lives. To keep more civilians from being caught in the crosshairs."

That's one way to look at it. "Yeah, I just... I didn't think it'd be this hard."

"Call her. Stop writing your fucking letters and pick up the phone and call her. You'll both feel a hell of a lot better after you talk to her."

"I can't," I say. I can't call her, but there are other people I *can* call. People who I know will be looking out for her. Firing up the computer, I find the number I need and dial it before I can talk myself out of it.

"This is Ash?" he answers.

"Ash, it's Noah Hunt. I'm... ah..."

He cuts me off before I can think of how to introduce myself to my future fucking brother-in-law. "I know who the fuck you are. You're the asshole who left my little sister in fucking tears."

"Yeah, I am."

"What do you want, Hunt?"

"I want to know if she's okay?" What did I really think I'd get out of this?

"She told me she's buying a cat and giving up on love forever. That her heart's fucking shattered into a million pieces. What the fuck do you think? *Is she okay?* Seriously, Hunt, if you don't come back and fucking fix this for her I will find you, rip your fucking heart out, and hand deliver it to her in a box. Then watch as she stomps all over it," he says.

"Well, that's..." *Graphic.* "It doesn't matter because I have every intention of coming back to her. Just... tell her..."

"Why don't you tell her yourself? If you can call me, then you can fucking call her."

"If I call her, she'll worry more than she already is. Don't tell me you can't hear the shit happening here."

"Noah, I've never seen my sister this fucking sad. I don't like it when my sister is sad. And I guarantee if I don't see her happy again real fucking soon, you won't like what happens." With that final threat, he hangs up.

"Fuck!" I throw the brick of a phone off the table.

"Hunt, everyone needs to use that fucking thing. If you break it, I'll break your kneecap," Hugo grunts.

"I'd like to see you try." I pick up another beer, grab my rifle, and walk out of the comms tent. I need some fucking air. It's dark out, but this place is still lit up like it's fucking daylight. I find a seat and stare at the moon.

I wonder what she's doing right now. I close my eyes, block out the sounds and the smells, and imagine I'm at our spot. Looking out into the darkness. Watching our future play out. Watching her dance.

19

Two weeks after Christmas

My fingers tighten around the wheel. It takes extra effort to keep my breathing normal. *Breathe in, breathe out.* It's all going to be okay.

No, it's not. It's never going to be okay again. Noah is gone, and I have ten pregnancy sticks—all flashing two pink lines at me—currently stashed in my closet.

I've worked my arse off the last few weeks. I've distracted myself with dance. Noah who? That's been working... until this morning when I woke up and realised I was two weeks late for my period. I rushed out to the chemist. The woman behind the counter looked at me with so much pity in her eyes.

What am I going to do? Oh my God, what are my parents going to say?

"What's wrong, Ava? Is this still about that Hunt asshole?"

Yes. Yes, it is! I want to scream at Axel. I want to shout and lose my mind. But that's not me. I'm controlled, planned, organised. I'm the good girl who never finds herself in these types of predicaments. Or at least I was...

What would Noah think of this? It's not as if I can call him and be like: *Hey, so remember that one time? Well, turns out, it does only take one time to knock me up.*

This is as much my fault as it is his. I can't put the blame on him. What I can blame him for is not freaking being here when I need him the most.

"I'm fine," I tell Axel, pulling into the carpark of my aunt and uncle's gym.

My brother turns to face me. "You know you're better than him anyway, Ava." With that little tidbit of advice, he jumps out of the car.

But I'm not better than him. I'm better *with* him.

With him in the audience. Watching me. No matter how much I've pushed myself these last two weeks, I can't get my routine flawless. I've been taping my feet and ankles, taking notes on where I need to improve. It's never good enough.

I drive aimlessly through the city. I need a plan. I can do this. I just need a plan. I need some time to think. Time alone.

I find myself in the underground carpark of Noah's building. Did he take my ID off the elevator before he left? Would he want me visiting his place? I should have offered to water his plants or something.

I walk over to the elevator and hold my breath as I press my thumb to the panel next to the letter P. The elevator starts its climb to the top, and the breath I was holding releases as a relieved huff. The moment I enter the penthouse, an indescribable rage overtakes me.

I'm angry that he left. I'm angry that I now have to figure out what to do on my own. I'm angry that I miss him so much. I feel sick every morning when I wake up as the reality that I have to face another day without him sinks in. I'm just angry all the time.

I don't know what comes over me as I pick up a crystal vase from the entry table and throw it against the wall. The glass shatters into tiny pieces. I look down and wonder if that's what my heart looks like. Just shattered pieces of something that used to be whole. As much as I want to start raging and destroying this whole place, I don't. I walk to the laundry in search of a dustpan and broom. I'm the good girl. Remember?

I hear the elevator's bell ring when I'm on my way back from the laundry, and my heart stops. *He's back?* I drop the dustpan and broom and run out into the foyer.

Shit... I stop in my tracks. It's not him. The man standing in front of me is most certainly not Noah. He's wearing a leather vest. He has tattoos all over him. Even on his neck.

We stare, each sizing the other up I guess, for what seems like forever.

"Ava, what happened here? Are you okay?" Brent finally asks me.

I laugh. I haven't actually seen Brent since he was at school with Noah. I never really knew him then either—just knew *of* him—and now he's talking to me like we're old pals?

My laughter comes out louder and harder. I can't stop it. Brent cautiously approaches me, as if he's afraid I might bite or something. "Did I miss the joke?" he questions.

I immediately pause. "Am I okay? Let's see... My boyfriend, who promised me he wouldn't leave, who promised he was getting out of the freaking military, decided to up and deploy. Am I okay? No, I'm not freaking okay." My words get louder and louder.

"He didn't leave you. He's doing his job, Ava. He'll be back."

"He's gone off to God knows where, doing God knows what. Everyone needs to stop telling me that he'll be back. That everything will be okay. It's not okay. It's never going to be okay." This time my voice is quiet as I struggle to hold the tears at bay.

"He's fine, and there's nothing in this world that can stop him from coming home to you, Ava." Brent sounds so sure of his statement. As if it's fact, rather than wishful thinking.

"You know what *can* stop him, Brent? A bullet, a missile rocket launcher, or whatever it is they call those things. A freaking bomb. A plane crash. So many bloody things can stop him from coming back."

"Right. Come with me." Brent walks down the hallway.

"Where are you going? And why are you here? Do you always come and raid Noah's place when he's away?" I follow the biker down the hall, and he just laughs.

"I'm here because your boy asked me to get something and deliver it to you. I got held up a little, but better late than never, right?" He shrugs as he moves some books off the shelf.

"What? You spoke to him? He called you?" I fall onto the sofa. If he called Brent, then why the hell can't he pick up the phone and call me?

"Two weeks ago. Like I said, I got held up, otherwise you would have had this sooner." Brent struts over, holding out a yellow envelope. The kind meant for documents.

"I don't want it." I shake my head. Whatever's in there, I don't want to see it.

"Tough. Noah was very insistent on you having this, so either you're going to open it or I'll do it for you."

"Why would he call you and not me?" I ask him, unable to keep the tears back any longer.

Brent curses under his breath. "Fucking Hunt." He squats down in front of me. "Look, Ava, I don't know why he hasn't called you. What I do know without a shred of doubt is that he loves you."

I shake my head, even though I know it's the truth.

"Ava, look at me. He has been fucking obsessed with you since we were in high school. He *is* coming back. He has to." Brent pushes to his feet. "I'm gonna get a drink. You want one?"

I shake my head again, before I stand and walk into Noah's bedroom. It still smells like him in here. Sitting on the bed, I pull the papers out of the envelope. They appear to be a bunch of legal documents and bank account numbers. The paper on top has my whole body shivering.

It's his will. Noah left me a copy of his will. I skim through the contents. "What have you done, Noah?" I whisper as I continue to read.

He's left everything to me. Everything he owns.

Everything. I don't want his stuff. I don't want his bloody bank accounts. I want him.

I pick up the next paper in the pile. It's an entire stack with more legal jargon, but it's clear what it is when I read the big bold letters: *trust account of Ava Williamson*. I almost fall off the bed when I see the numbers. Ten billion dollars.

He's left me a trust account with ten billion dollars in it. So I do what any sane person in my position would do. I rip it up. I tear the document to shreds. "I don't want your bloody money, asshole. I want you! I just want you," I scream into the empty room.

Brent stands in the doorway. "Is there someone I can call, Ava? Someone who can help you?"

"You can call Noah—get him here so I can throw his stupid will in his stupid face." I fall back onto the bed. Wrong move. My head lands on his pillow. It smells like him. "I'm fine, Brent. You don't have to stay here. I'll be fine. I'm going home soon anyway," I lie. I'm not fine.

"Yeah, I may be an arsehole, Ava, but I'm not that kind. I'm not about to leave you alone like this."

"I'm just going to close my eyes... rest for a bit," I say, tucking my face into the pillow. I haven't been sleeping properly since he left. I just need a little nap, then I'll get up and go to the dance school.

20

Noah

I've been trying to call Brent for the last two weeks to find out if Ava got that package I asked him to deliver. His phone's been going straight to fucking voicemail.

Today though... today it actually fucking rings.

"Noah, I'm going to fucking murder you in your sleep when you get home," he hisses down the line.

"Why the fuck are you whispering? And what'd I

do to piss you off this time? I'm not even in the same country."

"Guess where I am?"

"I don't know, asshole. I don't have time to play *Where's Waldo.*"

"I'm in your apartment. And guess who was here when I walked through the fucking door?" he asks.

I don't need to guess. There's only one person other than Brent who has access to that apartment. "Ava's there? How is she?"

"I swear to God, Noah, if you don't come home to this girl *and soon*, I don't think you're going to have a girl to come home to."

"What do you mean?"

"I mean, your girl looks like she needs to be kept on fucking suicide watch. Like she hasn't eaten or slept for weeks. She's laughing one minute, screaming at me the next, and then crying between."

"What? Make her fucking eat something, Brent," I tell him.

"Yeah, sure, I'll get right on that." His sarcasm drips through the receiver.

"Did you give her the envelope?"

"Yep."

"And...? Did she open it?"

"Yep. Your girl is probably the only person I know who would throw away ten billion dollars. She yelled a few choice words aimed at you as she shredded the trust fund papers you left her. And your will, idiot. Are you that fucking dumb? You left her a copy of your fucking will when you're off in a warzone?"

"She needs it, in case..." I can't finish the sentence.

"No. There is no *in case*. Get your fucking arse home, Noah," Brent yells. "And why haven't you fucking called her?"

"I can't. I don't want her to hear this shit. She doesn't need to know how bad it is..."

"How bad is it?" he asks, right as the air raid sirens go off in the background.

"I gotta go. Just look out for her for me. Please."

"You know I'm a sucker for a damsel in distress."

I can hear his grin. I hang up, refusing to take the bait.

"Time to roll, Hunt." Hugo slaps me on the back as he jogs out of the tent.

I'm right behind him. "What do you mean *time to roll*? We're not moving ahead until next week."

"Yeah, about that... CO says it's now or never. So I guess it's now. We've got ten minutes to be on that chopper," Hugo calls out to the rest of us.

I eye the Black Hawk. Fuck. My heart rate picks up as I run back into the tent and grab my gear. All five of us are scrambling around and strapping up.

"We know this. We've got this, boys. Don't let the fact that we're going in early distract you from the mission," one of the older guys, Gary, says. This might be my first mission; it's not anyone else's though.

All I can think as I sprint towards the dust being

kicked up by the spiralling blades is that I should have fucking called Ava. What if I don't make it out? I should have fucking called her, begged her to forgive me.

I shake my head and sit with my back against the hard metal. Hugo is yelling out the mission plan one last time, making sure we all know our orders. We're going to be dropped into the city. From there, we have an armoured vehicle ready that will transport us the remaining forty klicks to our target.

The chopper idles on a nearby rooftop. We all hop out and I watch it take off again. I follow my team into the building.

"Watch your six, boys. Let's roll."

We're in formation as we make our way down the stairs of this building. We've trained for this. It should be like second nature. But my heart is still pounding out of my chest. There's a lot of screaming, a lot of crying. I'm in the middle, with three of our guys to the front of me and two to the back—my CO at the lead, watching for an ambush. We make it to the vehicle in under five minutes. The bumpy drive is quiet. Sombre.

I guess we all have our own way of dealing with the stress of what we're about to do. I'd be lying if I said I wasn't fucking sweating balls right now. I can't even fucking close my eyes and see her. So I mentally prepare myself for what we're about to do, as I watch the city disappear behind us. I run through all the plans. All the discussions. All the possible scenarios in my head. We've been over this with a fine-tooth comb. We know what we're doing. And in an hour—tops—this mission will be completed and then we can fly out of this fucking desert.

We stop four klicks from our objective. We're boots to the ground the rest of the way. It's dark. We don our NVGs and slink towards the back of the enemy compound. Hugo guides us, silently signalling our directives. We're just about to jump the wall when we're hit with a barrage of bullets, rounds raining down on us like a torrential downpour.

"Fuck!" We all brace against the wall, taking cover wherever we can. I look to my right. Ken's laid out on the ground. I look left. "Cover me!" I yell over the white noise.

"What the fuck, Hunt. Stay fucking put."

Yeah, not gonna happen.

I make a run for it around the corner without getting hit. From this vantage point, I have a fucking perfect shot of one of the rooftop combatants. I don't think. I just do. Every bit of training I've endured has been for this moment. As soon as I take the first shot, I aim my sights on the next, then the next. I get five of them before they're zeroing in on my location. Ducking back down, I peer around the corner. Hugo and the boys have dragged Ken up against the wall.

"What do we do here, boss?" I ask.

"Stick to your orders. Get the job done. I don't

know about you, boys, but I'd like to fucking go home sometime this month," Hugo grunts.

We toss smoke grenades over the wall, wait ten seconds, and follow. We stick to formation, as we take out the fuckers surrounding us, and make our way to the door. Kicking it in, I enter first, clearing the room with two head shots.

"Clear," I call out as I continue through the building. We know where this cockroach is hiding. I retrace the map that's been ingrained in my subconscious, as we navigate through the chaos to our objective location without further fanfare.

I look back at the others. Surely I'm not the only one who thinks this was too fucking easy. When the rest of my team appears unfazed, I shake off the feeling in the pit of my stomach and kick in the second door. And as soon as it swings from the hinges, I realize why it was too fucking easy.

Our target is standing right there. In the middle of the room. Wearing a fucking suicide vest, his thumb pressing down on a red button wired around his hand and arm.

"Fuck, retreat, retreat!" I yell right as I watch the fucker lift his thumb.

21

One week later

I feel like I'm trapped in a really bad soap opera and I can't find the stage exit. I had everything planned out. And now those plans are just gone...

I don't know what to do. I haven't told anyone that I'm pregnant, not my parents nor my brothers. I can't exactly tell Noah either because I haven't freaking heard from him in four weeks.

Four weeks, two days, five hours. Not that I'm keeping count.

I've attempted to lose myself in ballet over the past few days. I know I won't be able to keep dancing, but I will make the most of it while I can.

Strangely enough, Axe has been hovering over me. And Ash keeps calling, although his own life just got a hell of a lot more complicated with the arrival of a baby and his public claim of Breanna McKinley. I'm surprised he's still breathing, really.

Breanna's family is crazy. I know that because my Aunt Ella married Dean McKinley, the only sane one in the bunch. Then they had Dom, and he's definitely inherited more from the McKinley side of his blood-line than the Williamson.

Ash is calling for the tenth time today. I've been avoiding going to see him. I know I'm the world's shit-tiest aunty right now. But if I spend any amount of time around my family, they're going to be able to tell that I'm barely keeping it together. I send his call to voice-mail. My phone rings again right away. I'm about to hit decline when I see Sophia's face.

"Hey, stranger," I answer in what I hope is a cheery tone.

"Hey, little dancer. How're things?" she asks.

I burst into tears. It's been weeks since I've spoken with her. She went to Canada with her family over

Christmas. "It's a mess, Soph. Everything is messed up," I cry, gaining the attention of some of the other dancers in the dressing room. So I quickly pick up my bag, walk out, and lock myself in my car.

"Ava, what happened? What's wrong? Shit, babe, what the fuck happened?" Her voice gets louder and louder, matching the volume of my sobs.

I try to relax, take a deep breath in and out, and count to ten. I do every relaxation technique I can think of. They aren't working. "Soph, I can't... I can't do it..."

"Ava, where are you? I'm coming now. Tell me where you are!" she screams. I can hear her engine starting up.

"I'm in my car, at the dance school," I push out between sobs.

"Okay, don't hang up. I'm coming. Who do I need to take a hit out on?" she asks.

"I can't do this. I don't know how to do this. This wasn't in the plan." I know I'm not making sense, but I ramble on anyway.

"Where's Noah? Want me to call him?"

I didn't tell her that he left just before Christmas. We've exchanged a few texts here and there, but I kept my misery to myself. "He... he left," I say.

"What do you mean he left? Where'd he go?"

"He got deployed somewhere. I don't know where he is... I can't contact him. He's gone, Soph, and I'm all alone. I can't do this."

"You are not alone, Ava. I'm here. I'll always be here. And I'm going to kick Noah's arse when I see him again."

Five minutes later, Sophia pulls up next to me in the carpark. She's knocking on my window. I barely get my door open before she's wrapping her arms around me.

"I'm sorry," I cry harder. I've been trying so bloody hard to hold it together. For weeks, I've been hiding my broken soul the best I could and now I feel like I've lost my will to fight.

"Shh, it's going to be okay. I've got you, babe. Come on, I'll take you home."

By the time Sophia parks in my driveway, I've managed to pull myself together a little. At least the tears have stopped. I grab her arm before she can get out of the car. "I'm pregnant," I blurt out and start sobbing all over again.

"Shit, fuck. Okay. It's okay, Ava. We've got this. We'll just adjust your plan. It's fine. We can do this." Her encouraging words don't match the look of sheer terror on her face.

"I can't do this. This isn't in the plan. Noah should be here. I need him," I choke on my grief, and my chest heaves to the point of being painful.

"I know, babe. I know. But you've got me, and you've got your family. And Noah's coming back, right? He'll be back. He's just... at work. When his shift finishes, he's coming back for you." Sophia takes my hand and leads me straight into my bedroom. "You're going to be okay. Whatever you decide to do, I'll be here. I'm not going anywhere."

"Thank you." I wipe the wetness from my cheeks. "How was Canada?" I ask her, needing to change the subject. At least for a bit.

"Cold," she deadpans.

I laugh. I didn't realize just how much I've missed her.

"We need snacks—*ice cream*. Find a movie. We're going to binge out for a few hours, then we're going to make adjustments to that plan of yours." She points to the whiteboard on my wall with my future written out in thick black marker.

The plan was to get into The Australian Ballet and become a prima ballerina. Travel the world and dance on all of the famous stages. Then I met Noah, and my plan changed to moving into his penthouse, dancing for The Australian Ballet, and eventually marrying him. The plan didn't include him leaving. The plan didn't include me becoming an unwed teenage mum.

"Okay, I'm just going to freshen up real quick." I shut myself into my bathroom. Splashing water on my face, I stare at my reflection in the mirror. I look like shit. There are dark circles under my now puffy eyes, and my skin is blotchy. I pull out some concealer and foundation powder. This is something I can control. I might be broken on the inside, but I don't have to show it on the outside.

I exit the bathroom to find Axel and Sophia arguing about something in the middle of my bedroom. Dizziness washes over me and I grab onto the dresser to keep myself upright. A sharp pain radiates through my stomach, causing me to bend at the waist as I grip my abdomen.

"Soph?" I call out to get her attention.

"Fuck, Ava, what the fuck? What's wrong?" Axe is by my side in seconds, holding me up.

I look from him to Sophia. "Something's wrong, Soph," I tell her.

"Shit, Axe, we need to get to the hospital *now*." She picks up her keys and starts for the door.

"The hospital? What the fuck for? Ava, what's going on?"

I scream as the pain tears through my body again. I've had horrible period cramps before, but this is like something is literally ripping me apart.

"She's fucking pregnant, Axe. Get her in the car now," Sophia yells at him.

My brother looks at me, his mouth opens and closes a few times, before he finally scoops me up bridal-style and runs us down the stairs. "Shit, fuck. What do I do, Ava? I should call Mum and Dad," he says as he sits in the back seat with me.

"Don't you dare call them. They're having a weekend away." I don't want to ruin my parents' weekend escape. I also don't want to face them right now. I don't want to see the disappointment in their eyes when they realise how badly I've messed up.

"Shit." Axe pulls at his hair as Sophia drives through the streets like a lunatic. Probably breaking every road rule.

I'm bent over, trying not to scream. I don't notice that Axe is on his phone until it's too late. "Ash, meet us at the emergency room—it's Ava." He listens to whatever Ash says back to him and pulls the phone away from his ear before replying, "I don't fucking know. She's fucking pregnant. Get to the fucking hospital, Ash. What am I supposed to do here?"

We pull up to the emergency department, and everything happens so fast. I'm being placed on a bed, people are all around me, and then everything starts to fade out.

WHY IS the alarm going off? Why does my room smell like antiseptic? I slowly open my eyes. Shit...

I sit up quickly, and regret it immediately as dizziness takes over. I lie back down and groan. What happened?

"Ava, sweetheart? How're you feeling?" Ash. Ash is here. I look over and see the stress and worry written all over his face.

"What happened?" I verbalize the question out loud this time.

"Sophia and Axel brought you here. You were in pain. Why didn't you tell me you were pregnant?" He sounds more hurt than angry over the fact that I didn't come to him first when I found out that I was...

Wait... I am still pregnant, aren't I? "Oh my God, is it...? The baby? What happened?" I ask again.

"You're okay. The doctors said everything looks good. The baby is okay."

I sigh in relief.

"They also said that you were dehydrated and more than likely suffering from some sort of extreme exhaustion."

"It's my fault." I've been pushing myself so hard with dance, trying to forget my problems, that I could have lost my child. I may not know how I'm going to cope with having a baby, but I do know that I don't want to lose it either. This little thing growing inside me is a piece of Noah. It's our love.

"It's not your fault. And I'm going to fucking kill that boyfriend of yours," Ash grunts.

"Noah left me, remember?" I remind him.

Ash looks torn, like he wants to tell me something but also doesn't. He runs a hand through his hair as Axe walks in and sighs. "You're awake—*thank God*. I thought you were going to leave me with this one as my only sibling. Could you imagine?" He ducks the slap Ash has aimed at his head.

"Where's Soph?" I ask.

"She's sleeping in the waiting room. She's been up all night, waiting for you to wake up."

"All night? How long have I been here? What time is it? I have to get to dance..." As I'm trying to push myself out of bed, Ash growls.

"Lie the fuck down, Ava. You're not going anywhere," he says, pacing the room.

"You're not my father, Ash. You can't tell me what to do." It's my retort for whenever one of my brothers likes to get bossy with me.

"No, but *I* am. Anyone want to tell me what the fuck is going on? And why your sister's laid up in a hospital bed and not one of you bothered to call me?" Dad walks into the room with Mum right behind him.

"Zac, calm down," she says quietly, before shoving past him and rushing to my side. "Baby, what happened? Are you okay? What'd the doctor say?" My mum grabs the chart from the end of the bed and starts reading it.

Oh no, are the walls moving? Why does it feel like the walls are suddenly closing in on me?

"Shit." My mother looks up from the clipboard to me. Though I don't see the disappointment I was expecting, I do recognize the concern and unshed tears in her eyes. "Axe, get Uncle Bray here," she directs to my brother.

"Ahh, okay." Axe walks out of the room with his phone to his ear.

"Sunshine, what's wrong? What is it?" Dad asks, attempting to take the chart from her hands.

"Zac, I need you to sit down. I need you to just sit down." Mum hugs my chart to her chest. She shares a look with Ash, who still appears as if he wants to commit murder, although now I think he's about to have an accomplice.

"Someone needs to tell me what the fuck is going on. Ava, sweetheart, whatever it is I'll fix it, baby. I promise." Dad sits on the edge of the hospital bed.

I shake my head, tears running down my face. "You can't fix this, Dad."

"Zac, she's pregnant," Mum blurts out.

I watch the shock shoot across my dad's face before he wipes it of all emotion. "No, she's not." He stands and straightens his suit jacket.

"Yes, I am," I tell him.

"No, you're eighteen, Ava. You're still a fucking child. You are not pregnant." His voice booms and bounces off the walls of the small room.

"Zac, you need to calm down." Mum takes hold of his hand.

"Calm down? Sunshine, my baby is... is..."

I sink into the bed as much as I can. I need to get out of this room. I can't deal with this. I hate that I've disappointed my parents. And I hate that Noah isn't here to bloody help me.

"Okay, either you calm the fuck down or you get out. Ava is in this bed due to stress. She doesn't fucking need you putting any more on her," Ash finally speaks up. And my dad now appears as though he'd have no qualms about killing his firstborn.

"Ash, you're not helping," Mum hisses.

"You know I'm right, Mum. She doesn't need stress. She needs to know that she's going to be okay. That we're all going to help her through this, and with whatever *she* decides to do." He puts extra emphasis on the fact that it's my choice. I've never been more appreciative of my brother than right now.

"Ava, Baby. You know I'm going to do whatever I have to do to help you." Dad lowers himself back down on the bed, by my feet. "But I am going to fucking kill that boyfriend of yours," he grunts.

22

Ava

The last week has been almost unbearable with my entire family hovering over me. Don't get me wrong, I appreciate their support and I know how blessed I am to have a family with so much love. Even if that same love can be suffocating.

I just need some time alone. Which is why I've made an escape. I had Sophia pick me up and told my parents we were going to lunch. I don't know why I came here. There is just something comforting about being in Noah's apartment. When I finally decided enough was enough and that I wanted to get away from everyone, this was the only place I wanted to be. The fact that I know no one else can get up here to bother me helps. All I want to do is lie down and sleep for a while.

There's a pile of mail on the entry table where I placed my handbag. The one sitting on top is addressed to me. Why do I have mail addressed to me here? Picking it up, I turn it over. Noah. It's from Noah. I quickly rummage through the stack of envelopes to see if there're any more and find a second one with my name on it in the pile. I've been carrying the letter he left with my Christmas gift in my bag for the last six weeks. I've read it so many times I have it memorised.

I take the two envelopes into his bedroom and place them on the bed. I walk into his closet and pull a t-shirt off the hanger. Stripping off my clothes, I leave them in a pile on the floor, throw on the t-shirt, and climb beneath the covers. As soon as my head hits the pillow, I inhale. He's everywhere. I open the first letter, and the moment I start reading it, the tears begin to flow—I'm surprised I have any left at this point. I've cried more in the past couple of months than I have in eighteen years. Or at least it feels like I have...

I finish the letter, then immediately rip into the next one.

DEAR AVA,

The days are so fucking long. Your face, knowing that I have you to come home to, that's what gets me through.

At least I fucking hope I have you to come home to. I know you're pissed at me, babe, but this trip isn't going to last long. I'll probably be home before you even read these letters.

Do you remember the spot I took you to, on that first night? You asked me what I saw when I looked out into the darkness. I told you I saw peace. What I should have told you... What I was too afraid to tell you at the time was that I saw you. When I look out into the nothingness so full of potential, I can see you. I see you dancing. I see you smiling. Laughing. I see you in a white dress. I see you as a mother to our children. I see our future.

Peace. You are my peace. A, you are everything that matters to me. I know you probably can't believe that right now, because I'm not there. But it's the truth. I fucking love you. In this life and the next.

Don't give up on us, A. We will have our future.

Always yours,

Noah

. . .

I WONDER how he's going to feel about me being the mother to his children now that it's actually happening.

I MUST DRIFT off to sleep, because I wake with a start when I hear someone riffling through the closet.

"Noah?" I call out. Is he home? Am I dreaming?

I get up and walk towards the sound. Yes, I'm aware this is exactly how the girl always gets herself killed in all the horror movies, but there are only a few people who have access to this apartment. I push the door open and Brent freezes. His eyes widen as they rake along the length of my body.

"What are you doing?" I ask. I mean, it's obvious he's putting a heap of Noah's clothes into a bag. But why?

"Ah, Ava, any chance you can just climb in that bed, forget you saw me, and go back to sleep?" He smirks as he continues packing.

"Brent, I know you're not that hard up for cash that you need to come in here and steal Noah's clothes. So, why exactly are you packing a bag of his things?" I ask.

"Ava, I'd love to stick around and chat but I gotta run. Things to do; people to see." Brent walks past me.

I practically jog to keep up with him. "People like Noah?" I ask. And his step falters, ever so slightly.

"Where is he, Brent? You know where he is... so tell me?"

"I have no idea. Last I heard, he was overseas." He jabs at the button for the lift while cursing under his breath.

"Please, just tell me. I know you know, and there's something I... I need to talk to him. Even if he doesn't want to see me afterwards, I need to talk to him," I plead as Brent steps onto the elevator.

"Look, I like you. And I fucking love him. You're a smart girl with resources, Ava. Use them. But I can't tell you. I wish I could." The doors close, effectively ending our conversation.

Noah is here, somewhere. If that's true, then why isn't he home? He doesn't get along with his family. There is no way he would go to his parents' place. The only other relative that he talks to is his cousin, Jhett.

I run back to the bedroom and call Axe. At the same time, I pick up my tights and pull them up my legs. "Ava, where the fuck are you? Everyone's looking for you," he yells.

"I'm fine. I'm at Noah's apartment. I need a favour."

"What do you need? And are you sure you're okay?"

"Noah's back," I blurt out.

"He's there? With you?"

"Well, no. But he's back. I know he is. I need you to call your friend Jhett and find out where he is."

"I'm going to fucking kill him. I'll find him and then I'll kill him," he seethes.

"Axe, no. Just get me an address. I don't understand why he wouldn't come home. Why wouldn't he call me? It doesn't matter. I need to see him."

"Okay, give me five. I'll call you back." Axe cuts the line.

I pace the entire apartment, looking from room to room. I don't know what I'm expecting to find. It's not like Noah's just going to jump out of the shadows. Five minutes—who would have thought that could feel like an eternity? By the time my phone vibrates in my hand, I've prepared myself for every worst-case scenario.

"Axe, did you find out?" I answer.

"Not exactly. I'm on my way to you. Meet me at the front of the building."

"Why? What do you know?"

"Just meet me out front, Ava." He cuts the call again. Shit. What could he possibly have learned that would make him drive over here?

"Where the bloody hell are you, Noah Hunt?" My scream echoes back at me. I might just wring his neck myself when I find him. He obviously doesn't want to find me. Well, fuck him. He's going to see me and hear me out one last time, whether he likes it or not.

Axe is already waiting for me when I exit the building. "Are you actually sober enough to drive?" I ask. He's had a licence for about five months, and I've seen him drive his car about five times. He's always opting for Ubers or making me play taxi.

"Yep. Get in." He shuts the door behind me and jogs around to the driver's side.

"Where are we going? What did you find out?"

He looks over at me. I can see the pity in his eyes. But he doesn't say anything.

"Axe, what did Jhett tell you?" I plead with him.

"Fuck, Ava, I don't... I'm sure Noah is fine. Jhett just said that there was an incident overseas, and Noah was flown back here. Two weeks ago. He's in the hospital but he wouldn't fucking tell me which one or what happened..."

"He's..." I choke on the sob that forms in my throat. Noah was in an accident. Two weeks ago. Why didn't I know? Why didn't anyone tell me?

"We're going to find him, Ava. We'll just go to the hospital and ask reception what ward he's on. Which hospital, I don't know, but we can stop at every single one in this fucking city until we find him." Axe reaches over and holds my hand. "It's okay. I'm sure he'll be fine. Jhett didn't sound all that worried."

I take out my phone. There's one person I know who can always track down anyone and get information when needed. Joshua McKinley. So I call the man who's like an uncle to me.

"Ava, sweetheart, how you doin'?" he asks, concern evident in his voice.

Great, he knows. I look to Axe. *Does everyone know*

that I'm pregnant? "Ah, I'm good, Josh. But I need a favour. Can you find out what hospital and what room someone is in for me?"

"I can. Is it the guy who's about to be pig food, Ava?" he responds.

I laugh a little. It's always been a joke in the family that Josh feeds anyone who crosses him to his pigs. Sometimes I'm not really sure it's a joke, though. "Ah, no. Please, Josh, I really need this one."

"Okay, sweetheart. What's the name?"

23

I close my eyes in an attempt to block out the world. But all it does is put me right back there. In that hallway. In front of the man wearing a suicide vest. Engulfed by the heat of the explosion.

"Fuck!" I yell, opening my eyes. I can't escape it. There's no fucking escape.

I try to sit up and everything fucking hurts. I'm hooked up to a multitude of machines, wires attached to random parts of my body. There's a lot of shit I don't remember. Like why I was there... How I ended up here, in this hospital... But the explosion? Every time I fucking close my eyes, I see it.

A nurse comes running in. "Mr Hunt, is everything okay?" she asks, checking the monitors as she enters. I don't bother answering her. Stupid questions don't deserve a fucking answer.

Is everything okay? *No, it's fucking not.*

They say I was lucky. That if I'd been seconds slower, I'd be coming home in a box. I came to a couple of days ago. They kept me in a medically induced coma for almost two weeks. I woke up in this fucking hospital room. Brent was sleeping in a chair in the corner. The doctors have been in and out, explaining all of the surgeries I've undergone. The recovery plans I'm looking at. But the one thing they all keep repeating is just how *lucky* I am that I'll make a full recovery. Right now, I don't feel lucky. I feel like fucking shit. I feel like I've been hit by a freight train.

Brent walks back into the room carrying a bag. He throws it on the ground in the corner. He hasn't left since I first woke up. He's been camped out in this room with me, until I sent him out to get me clothes. Not that I can fucking move enough to put them on. I have a fractured femur bone. A few broken ribs. My left shoulder's dislocated. They've put a metal rod in my leg. And I can't even fucking stand to take a piss.

"She was there," he says.

"Who was there?" I ask, confused.

"Ava. She was there, at your apartment."

Huh... He asked if I wanted him to call Ava after I first woke up. When I looked at him blankly, with no clue as to who he was fucking talking about, his whole face paled. He spent all yesterday telling me stories about our senior year. Some of it I remembered; some of it seemed like someone else's life entirely. I remember ballet. I remember watching ballet. But that's all I've got.

Then he tried to get me to remember her. Ava. He says she's my girlfriend. But I can't for the life of me conjure up a picture of her face. Every time I've tried, I've come up blank. How important can she be if I can't remember her? Brent must be thinking she's something she's clearly fucking not.

"Why would she be in my apartment?" I ask. I don't let anyone in my apartment.

"Oh, I don't know, lover boy. It might have something to do with the fact that—for her eighteenth birthday—you gave her a key to your penthouse."

"Now I know you're bullshitting me. They're no keys."

"You said the key was symbolic, asshole. You had her thumbprint put into the system."

"Have it removed. I don't want some chick I don't know going through my shit."

"Yeah, I'm not doing that. Because when your brain

catches up with the present, you'll fucking shoot me for taking that away from her."

"Doubtful." I close my eyes. *Ava*, I repeat the name over and over again in my head. And still there's nothing. Not a shred of recognition.

There's a lot of other shit I don't remember. Like joining the fucking Army. Getting deployed. I've had a few men in uniform come in, claiming to know me. But I have no fucking idea who they are. The doctors say the chances are high that I'll regain the memories I've lost. I just need to relax and give it time. But easier said than fucking done.

"Retreat. Retreat!" I hear my own voice calling out. Yelling. Right before I feel the explosion. The walls falling down around us and crushing me. I can make out some shouting, gunfire, and then nothing.

I was told the men dragged me out. That one of them carried me to the retrieval chopper. And I was told my quick reaction saved the lives of everyone in that hallway. I keep getting *told* shit. What I want to know is why? If I can't remember a single thing about her, why does the name *Ava* keep replaying in my mind? And why do I feel like I want to fucking watch the ballet?

I shake my head and open my eyes. Brent is glaring at me with a scowl. "She looked at me like I broke her fucking heart. Just so you know, next time she asks me where you are, I'm fucking telling her. Who knows?

She might be the key to getting you back." He reclaims his spot on the chair in the corner.

"I *am* fucking back. I'm here, aren't I?"

"Your body is. But where's your head at, Noah?" he asks.

I don't answer him. How can I? I don't fucking know where the fuck my head's at. All I know is the continuous pain, and the fucking fogginess of the meds that are doing a shitty fucking job of numbing it. "You try getting blown to pieces and then see how you come out of it," I grunt.

"Yeah, hard pass. Look, man, you know I have your back. Always. But you gotta let me call her, get her here." These repetitive conversations are getting irritating.

"Like I said the last hundred times, I don't want to see anyone, Brent. Especially not some chick I don't even fucking remember."

"Right, well, you better not fucking forget this was your call when you do fucking remember her," he grunts. We sit in a comfortable silence. Or at least everything on the outside is silent. Inside my head, it's anything but fucking quiet. I wish I could close my eyes, just for a little while, and find some fucking peace...

Peace. As soon as the word pops into my thoughts, I fucking see dancing again. I scour my brain in an attempt to figure out the jigsaw puzzle of images. What the fuck is with the dancing?

There's a commotion in the hallway outside my room. Brent's eyes widen as he looks at me. "Shit." He stands and peeks his head out the door before stumbling backwards as it slams open.

An angry-looking, petite blonde bombshell storms inside, poking Brent in the chest with her index finger. "I'm going to deal with you later. I can't believe you haven't called me. Why the bloody hell didn't anyone call me?" Her voice gets louder, and I groan. The noise hurts my fucking head. Her neck snaps in my direction and her face pales as she stares at me. "Noah?" she questions. "What the hell happened? Oh my God, I'm so sorry. I should have been here."

She rushes over to my side. Her hand laces with my fingers. And the moment her skin touches mine, something zaps up my arm. My eyebrows scrunch down in confusion. What the hell was that? Who the fuck is this girl?

"I'm so sorry. I would have come sooner. No one called me. Shit, are you okay? No, of course you're not okay. Look at you! Shit... I'm sorry I didn't say goodbye properly before you left. I should have been more understanding. It should have been different. And why the hell haven't you called?" She's rambling.

"Ah, Ava, there's something you need to know," Brent interjects, trying to get her attention.

So, this is Ava. I smirk. I can see how any guy could fall for this girl. She's fucking gorgeous. Even when she's spiralling. "Shut up, Brent. I don't want to hear anything you have to say. You had the opportunity to talk to me and you chose not to."

He holds his hands up in surrender.

"Ava, sweetheart, you should sit down," some young kid says from behind her. Where the fuck did he come from? And why is he calling her sweetheart?

"I'm fine, Axe. What did the doctors say? Doesn't matter. We can get a second opinion, Noah. I'll find the best specialists." She walks to the end of the bed, picks up my chart, takes out her phone, and snaps photos of each of the pages.

"What the fuck are you doing? Put that down," I hiss. That's a major invasion of privacy.

"I'm just going to send it to my mum. She'll know what it says better than I will."

"Look, Ava, you really should sit down." Brent snatches the folder out of her hands.

"Everyone needs to stop telling me what to do. I'm fine," she seethes. She looks anything but fine. I close my eyes and groan. I don't have the energy to deal with this shit. This girl needs to leave.

I open my mouth to tell her as much when all hell breaks loose. "He has amnesia, Ava. He doesn't know who you are," Brent says, at the same time the kid spits out, "You fucking knocked up my sister and left her alone. You're lucky you're already fucking laid out in a bed."

What the fuck?

"What do you mean he has amnesia? He remembers me. Noah, tell him you know who I am. You wouldn't forget me... you wouldn't." The girl's pleading eyes sear into mine.

"I-I'm sorry. I can't. I don't..." I admit. That's when she finally sits down.

"Oh, just perfect. Ava, let's go. This is a fucking joke. You're a fucking joke, Hunt." The kid tries to pull her up from the chair. But her eyes are trained on me, tears running down her face. "Ava, this isn't good for you. We need to go before you end up in a hospital bed again." The kid tries to urge her to leave.

"Why were you in a hospital bed?" I ask her, though I have no idea why I even care.

"I-I fainted. It's nothing. I'm fine," she says for what seems like the hundredth time.

"Stress. She's fucking pregnant and stressed the fuck out over your ass. That's why she fainted. Why she almost lost your baby."

Pregnant. There's that word again. She's pregnant. I look to Brent. He appears just as shocked and confused as I am. And he's the one with all his fucking memories.

24

Ava

All of the noise in the room fades out. Noah's looking at me like I'm a complete stranger.

He doesn't remember you.

No, I refuse to believe that. Noah wouldn't forget me. He wouldn't forget us. I don't know what to do. I can't move. I don't know what to say. What can I say?

Axe puts his arm around my shoulders, but my eyes stay locked on Noah's, whose own eyes flare with something as they focus on my little brother. I don't think it's jealousy I see there. I don't know what it is though.

"Ava, come on, you need to relax. Fuck, I should call Mum. She'll know what to do." Axe lets go of me and pulls out his phone. I nod my head but I'm not really paying attention to anything but the man in front of me.

"I think we all need to give Noah a breather. Come on, Ava, I'll shout you a shitty coffee from the cafeteria," Brent says.

I don't move. I still can't move. "Ah, you go ahead. Maybe... can you get me a water?" I ask him, shifting to the chair that's by Noah's bed.

"Noah, what do you want me to do here?" Brent says, ignoring my request.

He looks between Brent and me. I hold my breath, waiting for him to say something. "Go and get her a water," he finally answers.

"Okay, Axe, is it? You're coming with me," Brent orders.

That has me turning in their direction. I don't know Brent all that well. What I do know about him is he's the vice president of a biker club. And I don't need my little brother going anywhere with him. "No, Axe, you can leave me here. Go home," I tell him.

"I'm not leaving without you, Ava. I'll be outside." Axe shoves through the door.

"Right, I'll just go and..." Brent doesn't finish his

sentence; instead, he walks out of the room, shooting one last look from me to Noah.

The constant beeping of the machines is the only noise now. Noah and I sit here, staring at each other, not saying a word. After a few minutes, I break first. "I don't care," I say.

"You don't care about what?" he asks, his eyebrows drawn down.

"I don't care if you don't remember me, because I remember you. I remember everything. I can remember for both of us, Noah. It'll be okay. It's going to be fine." I'm not sure who I'm trying to convince.

"I'm sorry." He's quiet. "I can see how upset you are."

"What happened?" I ask.

"There was an explosion." His voice is terse and he looks away.

"Okay. I missed you so much." I wipe at the fresh tears running down my cheeks. Noah raises his eyes to me again but doesn't say anything. "What can I do?" I continue in an even tone. "What have the doctors said?"

"I... they say I have a traumatic brain injury. That it's possible I'll recover all of my memories with time. That I'm lucky." He grits his teeth on the last word.

"Lucky? Right. Well, it doesn't matter if you don't get your memories back, Noah. Because I'm going to make you fall in love with me again. I don't care how many hours I need to stand here and dance for you. I *will* make you fall in love with me again. I mean, you did it once, and I wasn't even trying back then."

"What did you say?" he asks.

"That I'll make you fall in love with me again?"

"No, not that. The dancing?"

"I'm a dancer. Or at least I was. You said the first time you saw me, I was dancing on stage and you've been in love with me ever since. Why?"

"I keep seeing a ballet dancer but I can't make out a face." He shrugs.

"You do remember." I jump out of my seat, then have to catch myself on the edge of his bed as dizziness has me hunched over and pausing. "Shit."

"Fuck, are you okay?" Noah yells. "Fuck!" His voice grows louder. I notice that his eyes are closed with his jaw clenched tight.

"I'm fine. I just got up too fast. I'm sorry."

"You need to be more fucking careful," he grits out.

I'm taken aback by his tone. I've never heard Noah talk to anyone in that tone before. "I-I'm sorry. I didn't... I'm sorry." I have no idea what to say.

"You should leave." He doesn't open his eyes.

"No." My fists clench at my sides.

"What do you mean *no*? You shouldn't be here. How much could I have possibly loved you if I can't even fucking remember you?" This time he does open his eyes, and all I see is anger and frustration staring back at me.

"Y-you don't mean that." My voice quivers.

"Look, I'm sure you're a nice girl and all, but you really do need to leave." He closes his eyes again, putting his head back against the pillow. Dismissing me.

"You know what? I'll think I'll stay if it's all the same to you. Oh, and not that you've asked but I'm guessing this baby—the one you and I created together —is due in roughly six months." I wrap my arms around myself. This isn't the time to crumble. He'll never admit it, but he needs me to be strong for both of us.

"Yeah, I'm going to need a DNA test on that one, sweetheart. You're not the first girl to try to claim a Hunt baby." He smirks.

The asshole smirks at me. I'm absolutely fuming. "You think I'd purposely get myself knocked up, at bloody eighteen. Ruin my dreams of dancing for The Australian Ballet? For what? The privilege of having a Hunt baby?"

"Like I said, you wouldn't be the first."

"Right. Tell me something, Noah, have you spoken to your lawyer since you've been here?"

"No, why?"

"You might want to get on that and change your bloody will. What the hell were you even thinking, leaving me everything? Do you know what kind of target that puts on my back? What your family would do to me?" I ask him.

"I left you everything?" he parrots.

"Yep."

"Huh." He smiles.

"What does that mean? *Huh*?"

"I either really fucking liked you or really fucking hated you, for me to do something like that."

"Loved. Love. You love me, Noah." I don't know what to do here. I need to talk to someone, a medical professional, a doctor. Anyone who can tell me what I'm meant to do. I pull my phone out of my pocket, about to call my mum, when there's a light knock on the door.

"Yeah," Noah calls out, groaning.

"What's wrong?" I ask him, though it's evident he's in pain.

"Nothing."

The door opens and I look behind me to see my mother walking in. "Ava, baby, I came as quick as I could."

I run over and wrap my arms around her. And I freaking cry. I can't seem to stop crying lately. I hate it. "He... he doesn't remember me, Mum," I manage to get out through my sobs.

"Oh God, I'm so sorry, baby." She hugs me tighter. "Ava, I know it's really hard, but you need to try to calm yourself. Take deep breaths. Sit down."

I let her lead me back to the chair closest to Noah. I take a seat and look up to see him watching us. Watching me. "You okay?" he asks.

"I'm fine," I bite out. I'm not fine. My boyfriend, my

soul mate, who I love with every fibre of my being, doesn't know who the hell I am. Oh, and I'm pregnant with his baby, and he thinks I'm just after his money. How could I possibly be fine right now?

"Hi, I'm Alyssa. Ava's mother." Mum smiles down at Noah.

He nods his head. "I'm sorry but I don't…"

"Oh, it's fine. We've actually never met. I do know your mother though. Is she here?" Mum asks.

"No, and I'd like to keep it that way," Noah answers.

"Okay, do you need anything?" Mum picks up the chart from the end of his bed and starts reading. She pauses to glance up at Noah. "I'm sorry. Old habits die hard, I guess," she says, dropping the clipboard back into the slot. "I used to be a nurse." She makes no attempt to stop prodding as she assesses each of the medical devices he's hooked up to. "How's the pain?" she continues.

"Tolerable." Noah grits his teeth and closes his eyes as he answers.

"Have the doctors spoken to you about your injuries? What the recovery will look like?"

"Yep."

"Okay, I understand that this is all overwhelming and having strangers in your room is probably not helping. So I'm not going to stick around. Ava, come walk me out." Mum smiles down at Noah. "It was nice meeting you, Noah. Welcome to the family."

25

I watch as Ava stands, and there's a niggling feeling in the pit of my stomach. I can't put a label on it though. It's like I want to grab her hand and keep her here. But that's ridiculous. I don't know her.

She picks up her phone and looks down at the screen. Then back at me. "I'll only be a minute, but here." She taps something, then hands the device to me. "Have a look through this album while I'm gone."

I take her phone but don't respond. An odd sense of relief washes over me with the knowledge that she isn't leaving for good. As soon as the door closes, I hold the device up to my face and see a photo. Ava and me, both of us with goofy smiles. I swipe my finger across the screen and continue swiping. There's an endless number of pictures. Some of just me, but most show us together.

I close my eyes, trying like hell to remember any of these times. I can't. "Fucking hell!" I scream.

Brent comes back into the room. He doesn't say anything. Just sits down. My hand clenches around the phone as I continue to stare at a photo of me and Ava. I look fucking happy. I don't remember ever being that happy. "Uncle Brent has a good ring to it, don't you think?" Brent finally breaks the silence.

"What the fuck are you talking about?"

"You went and got Ava Williamson pregnant, idiot. I'd like to think it was an accident but I know how fucking obsessed you are with that girl, so it really wouldn't surprise me if you did it on purpose."

"We don't know that it's mine. I told her that I wanted a DNA test."

"What the fuck, Noah? When have I ever fucking lied to you?" he asks.

"You haven't."

"Right, so listen to me very fucking carefully,

asshole. That girl is everything to you. One day you're going to remember, and then you're going to have a shit-ton of fucking self-pity going on."

I don't bother responding. I close my eyes and try to block everything out.

"*Retreat! Retreat!*"

I start running right as the explosion rings out. And the walls—the shrapnel—start falling down all around me. On me.

"Argh, fuck," I yell.

"Noah, wake up. Noah!" Someone is shaking me. That voice... the voice of an angel. But that can't be right. If I'm dead, I'm going down not up. "Noah, please open your eyes. It's just a dream."

I shove at the hand clutching my shoulder. My eyes burst open. I look around the room. "What? Where...?" I start to question and then it hits me. I'm in the hospital.

I look to the girl who's hovering above me. "Noah, it's okay. You're okay. It was just a dream."

"That's the thing. It wasn't..." I whisper.

We stare at each other and I let myself get lost in those ocean-blue eyes of hers. "Do you want me to call for a doctor? A nurse?" she asks.

I shake my head and try to relax my body. Everything fucking hurts. My ears won't stop fucking ring-ing. "Where's Brent?" I question.

"He said he'd be back tomorrow."

I nod my head. Great, I'm trapped in a room with a girl I don't know, but I'm supposed to love. A girl who's pregnant with my child—supposedly. What the fuck am I meant to say? I've got nothing. So I do my best to pretend. Pretend she's not here. Pretend that I can't fucking smell her. That my dick doesn't fucking harden whenever I look at her.

"You should go home. It's late," I tell her. She ignores me as she curls her slim body into the chair. She's too fucking thin. "Have you eaten?" I ask, at the same time I press the call button for a nurse.

"I'm fine," she says.

I've heard her say that a lot: *I'm fine.* I might not know this girl, but I do know that she's *not fine.* She's clearly not okay. And for some fucking reason that bothers me.

The nurse enters the room. "Mr Hunt, what can I do for you?"

"Can you arrange to have some food brought in for her." I nod my head towards Ava.

"You don't have to do that. I'm fine," Ava says to the woman.

"Just have some food sent in please," I instruct again. The nurse nods her head and walks out. "You know, people who say they're fine are usually anything but fine, babe," I say.

Ava stands and looks down at me in shock. "You're right. I'm not fine. I'm not okay. I'm holding on by a bloody thread here, Noah. But I will be fine. I will be okay." Her voice is not nearly as confident as her words are.

I want to offer her some encouragement. I want to promise her that it'll be okay. But I can't. I can't give her what she's looking for.

The nurse comes back in with a tray of fruit and sandwiches. She places it down on the table. "Is there anything else you need, Mr Hunt?"

"No, we're good," I say. Once the woman leaves the room again, I nod my head towards the tray. "Eat," I tell Ava.

"I'm not hungry." She sits back down, folding her arms around herself.

"Eat some fucking food, Ava," I yell, losing my patience and regretting it immediately. Fucking hell. I close my eyes. I can't see the hurt on her face.

"You can scream at me all you want, Noah. I can take it." Her voice is quiet. I know she's trying to be strong. But she's not.

"Just eat some food, please..."

"Fine, I'll have some fruit. I don't eat bread," she replies.

"One sandwich isn't going to kill you, Ava," I tell her.

My eyes pop open when she gasps. "What's wrong?" I ask, ready to call for the nurse again.

"I—you... it's nothing. You've said that to me before. The first time you took me to your apartment, you made me a sandwich and said that exact same thing."

"Huh, well, clearly I was right." I smirk.

Ava smiles a little before picking up the sandwich and taking a bite. I like her smile; she has a nice smile. We sit in silence as she eats and I lie in this fucking bed, unable to move. Unable to do fucking anything. My fists clench and unclench. I can feel the anger inside me. I can feel the need to fucking yell, scream, and throw shit. And there's not a single fucking thing I can do about it.

I haven't felt this hopeless since I was young and still living with my parents. The constant anger I had towards them for making me their fucking weapon against each other. For trying to turn me into one of *them*. Money hungry assholes with absolutely no morals. Full of fake smiles and an arsenal of knives ready to stab you in the back.

Ava's smile isn't fake. There isn't anything fake about this girl. How the fuck did someone like her get involved with someone like me? I want to ask her, but I don't. "How is it?" I say instead, gesturing to the sandwich.

"Nowhere near as good as the one you made me. But it's not bad."

I glance at her stomach. It's still pretty flat. It's hard

to believe she's pregnant. With my kid. "Is there anything you need? Have you seen a doctor?" I ask her.

"I have an appointment in two days. I don't need anything *from* you, Noah. All I need is you," she says, ducking her head down.

I don't know if I can give her that. "You're keeping it, right?"

"Of course I am," she huffs out, clearly offended by the implication. "I'll admit I wasn't sure at first. I'm eighteen, Noah. I had dreams. Goals. A plan. *We* had a plan. And a baby doesn't exactly fit into that plan. But then, when I thought I was going to miscarry..." She pauses, inhaling deeply. "I was terrified I was going to lose the only piece of you I'd ever have again."

I don't know what to say to that, but I like hearing her talk. I like talking to her. "Tell me about the plan? Our plan."

26

I jump up with a jolt. The screams, the sounds of agony, fill the room as I try to get my bearings.

"What the hell? Oh my God, Noah?" I'm at his side in an instant. His face is scrunched up in pain. I press the button for the nurse. "Noah, what can I do? Tell me what I can do?" I hold his hand. He squeezes mine so tight I'm afraid he's going to break my fingers. The door opens and a nurse rushes in. "You have to help him, do something," I yell at her.

"Mr Hunt, what's happening?" she asks casually as she messes with the machines and adjusts the monitors.

"What's happening? He's in bloody pain. Do something—give him something!"

"Look, miss, you're gonna have to leave if you can't compose yourself."

"Leave? I'd like to see you try to drag me outta this room. If you don't hurry up and help him, I'm gonna call the hospital's chief and have you bloody fired," I threaten her.

Noah looks up at me. "It's okay, babe. It's fine," he says.

"It's not fine, Noah. You're clearly in pain and she should be doing her bloody job."

"I'm sorry, Mr Hunt. You're not due for a top up of pain medication for another thirty minutes," the woman explains. And all I can think is how bloody useless she is.

"What? No, give him something now," I demand.

"It's fine. Thank you," Noah dismisses her. "Ava, you need to relax. Getting worked up can't be good for you." He smirks at me as he stares at my stomach.

"Relax, sure. I'll relax when this hospital finally employs some competent staff," I seethe.

Noah grins. "I can see how I could have fallen in love with you."

That stops me. For a moment, I forgot. I forgot that he doesn't know who I am. I forgot that he has no memory of us. But those words give me hope. He will fall in love with me again. I know he will. I smile down at him. "I'm very loveable, obviously."

"Obviously." His lips tip up. "Can I?" He rests his hand on my lower abdomen. "Does it feel different?"

"I'm nauseous seventy percent of the day. I'm tired, and my boobs hurt," I blurt out. That raises his eyes to my chest. He looks like he wants to say something, but he's holding back. "Just say it. Whatever depraved thought you're having and trying not to let on, just say it." I laugh.

"Well, I was just thinking I could, you know, always massage *them* for you. It could help?" he questions. Then immediately removes his hand from my stomach like I've burnt him. "I'm sorry... I shouldn't have said that."

"Trust me, it's far from the filthiest thing you've ever said or done to me. You do know your tongue has literally licked every inch of my skin."

His eyes roam up and down my body—well, the parts he can see without moving too much anyway. I recognize the lust in them. "Fuck, I really wish I remembered doing that," he grunts.

"Don't worry, as soon as we break you out of here, you can do it again." I lift one shoulder, like it's not a big deal. Like I'm not aching to have him touch me again. To have him worship me like he used to. I roll the kink out of my neck. This chair really wasn't the most comfortable place to sleep. I also probably look like shit. "I'm just going to take a quick shower— freshen up. Won't be long," I say, quickly shutting myself in the bathroom.

I lean against the door. Holy shit, I really am way out of my depth here. I just need to hold it together a little while longer. He's going to remember. And if he doesn't, he's going to love me again. There's no other option.

I let the tiny shower cubicle steam up and then step under the stream. I use the shampoo and conditioner provided by the hospital. I scrub myself with the lavender-scented bodywash. As much as I want to sit under the hot water and feel sorry for myself, I don't. I turn off the faucet and towel dry my hair before wrapping the scratchy material around my body. Then I pick up my pile of clothes from the floor. I don't want to put them back on. I open the door and spot Noah's bag in the corner. I know he has shirts and hopefully a pair of sweats in there that I can borrow.

"Nice shower?" he asks as I make my way across the room.

"It's nowhere near as good as yours." I pick up his bag and place it on the chair. Opening the zip, I start rummaging through the contents.

"Looking for something in particular?" Noah asks.

I glance back and smile at him. I don't miss how intently his eyes focus on my legs. I straighten up and raise to a three-quarter pointe before transitioning to a grand battement position. With one leg right up in the air, I hold my ankle near my ear and slightly pivot my waist to look at him.

His pupils are wide, his mouth gaping. "Fuck me," he says, trailing his gaze up and down my body. I'm sure from this angle he can see everything beneath the towel. I lower my leg, pull a shirt and a pair of sweats out of his bag, and turn back to face him.

"You really loved watching me dance," I tell him.

"I can see why."

We share a moment. At least I think it's a moment. My whole body tingles with excitement. With need. But that brief exchange is interrupted when Brent enters the room. "What's up, lovebirds?" he says, eyeing me from top to bottom.

"Brent, get the fuck out! Ava, get some fucking clothes on," Noah grunts, sending a death glare to his best friend.

"Chill, bro, it's cool. Ava, looking good, sweetheart." Brent winks at me.

"Ah, yeah, I'm just gonna..." I squeeze past him and shut myself in the bathroom for a second time.

I make quick work of getting dressed. I have to roll the sweats at the waist to keep them from sliding down. I look like shit, but it'll do. I run my fingers through my hair and tie it up in a messy bun on top of my head. I walk out of the bathroom and both men pause their conversation to stare at me. I peer down at myself. I know I look stupid in Noah's clothes, but do they really need to stare?

"What?" I ask.

"Brent, out," Noah growls.

"Why would I leave when the view in here is so spectacular?" Brent answers, winking at me. He struts to my side and throws an arm over my shoulder. "Maybe we should go get some breakfast, babe. Leave Noah here to rest a bit?"

"Ah, I'm not hungry," I tell him. Noah looks like he's about to burst a vein in his forehead. "Are you okay? That's a stupid question—of course you're not. Where the hell is that nurse? Surely it's time for your meds."

"Brent, how fond are you of your arm?" Noah is glaring at the biker.

"Well, I'm pretty attached to it. Literally."

"Then remove it from my fucking girl before I tear it off your body."

I shouldn't be giddy at Noah's threat to his friend. But that's exactly what I am. He just called me his girl. Does he remember? Please, God, let him remember.

"Wait, Noah, do you remember?" Brent verbalises the question that's stuck in my throat.

"No, but that doesn't mean I want you touching her. Remove your fucking arm," he repeats.

My heart deflates. Brent does as he's told but not before leaning down and whispering in my ear, "Don't give up on him, babe. He's definitely still a goner for you."

I reply with a little nod of my head. I will never give up on him. And I'll never give him up. I need him, more than I want to admit. I sit down and scroll through the thousands of notifications on my phone. There are messages from everyone. I reply to them all, letting them know I'm okay. Then I see one from my dad.

Dad: Sweetheart, I'm coming to the hospital this morning. I've got a bag your mother wanted me to give you.

"Shit!" I shriek.

"What's wrong? Ah, fuck!" Noah cries out in agony as he attempts to sit upright and reach for me.

"Don't bloody move." I press the button for the nurse.

"What's wrong?" Noah asks again through ragged breaths.

"My dad's coming here. This morning," I tell him.

er father's coming here? Why does she look so worried? From the way she and her mother interacted yesterday, I would have suspected Ava came from a good, loving family. The opposite of mine. I know my parents were notified of the incident. And of the fact that I'm here. Yet I haven't seen either of them step foot through that door.

"Ava, are you afraid of your father?" I ask her,

taking hold of her hand. And that zap runs up my arm again the instant our skin touches.

"What? No, of course not. My dad would never hurt me." She squeezes my palm. "You, on the other hand, he very much would. I'm not scared for me. I'm scared for you, Noah."

I laugh, or at least I try to, until it feels like every single one of my organs is tearing apart inside me. "Ah, fuck." I grit my teeth, close my eyes, and wait for the pain to pass. The thing is... it never fucking passes. I just try my best to get used to it. "Babe, I'm not sure there's much your father could do to hurt me any more than I already am at this point," I tell her.

She gets a starry-eyed look on her face. "Don't worry, Noah, I won't let anyone hurt you. Where the hell is that nurse? Brent, can you go get someone? He needs pain meds," Ava directs to my friend, who's trying hard not to smile.

"You know, most people lookin' to order me around learn the hard way that I don't listen." He folds his arms over his chest.

"I'm not ordering you, Brent. I'm asking you. Please, can you get someone?" Ava's voice turns saccharine sweet.

"Sure, babe. Whatever you say." He salutes her.

"It's Ava, not babe," she corrects him just as he reaches the door. Brent shakes his head and walks out.

"Ava, are you sure you're okay?" I draw her attention back to me.

She drops her gaze, her eyebrows drawn together. "I like it better when you call me babe." She smiles.

"Thank fuck, because so do I." I can't describe it... I don't think I'm in love with her, but I do feel something. I just don't know what it is. I wish I could fucking remember her. She seems like someone I'd like to be around a lot more.

I'm surprised she's still here, to be honest. Especially after she gave me a very detailed rundown of what *our* plan was *before* I deployed. How she was taking me home to meet her family for Christmas. How we were going to move in together. How she was supposed to audition for The Australian Ballet.

I felt her sadness when she talked about that part of the plan. I can see how much she wants that. She has so much passion for the ballet. I really do want to see her dance. I want to see her up on a stage. When she lifted her leg earlier, wearing nothing but a towel, I almost lost my damn mind. My cock hardened to the point of being painful. All I could imagine was burying my face between her thighs and tasting her, though something tells me one taste wouldn't be enough.

"I'm sorry." Ava sighs.

"For what?"

"For whatever my dad says or does. I'm sorry. I just want to get that out in the open. And it doesn't matter what anyone says. You and me, we are forever, Noah."

"I don't want you to get your hopes up, babe. I may never get my memory back. And I'm going to be stuck here for a while. I have more surgeries to go through. I don't expect you to stick around for all that..."

Ava's lips are on mine before I can blink. Her tongue slides along the seam of my mouth, seeking entrance. It's a soft kiss, but I can feel her love poured into it. All too soon, she pulls away.

"Sorry," she says.

"Don't be." My lips tilt up at her, as the nurse rushes into the room like she's being chased down by a bloody madman.

"I'm so sorry, Mr Hunt. Let's get you topped up," she says.

I hold on to Ava's hand while the nurse pushes morphine into the drip. Mostly because I like holding her hand, and partly because the way she's giving the older woman a death glare is honestly a little scary.

FOR THE FIRST time since finding myself in this bed, I don't wake up to the sound of my own screams. No, I wake up to hushed voices. I slowly open my eyes to see Ava talking to an older man. It takes a while for it to click that he must be her father. I quickly close them again. I know I should make it known that I'm awake. I don't know what has me wanting to listen to their conversation, but that's exactly what I do.

"I don't care, Dad. I love him. That's enough," Ava says.

"Ava, sweetheart, I'm not saying you can't support him. What I am saying is that you can't keep sleeping in a hospital chair. You should come home tonight. Have dinner with your family. Get a good night's sleep and come back in the morning if that's what you want to do," her dad argues. I can't deny that he's right. She shouldn't be sleeping in a chair.

"Noah is family, Dad. I'm not going anywhere until he does."

"You know, I used to think your stubborn streak was adorable. Now I just find it fucking annoying." His tone isn't harsh. He sounds almost like he's joking with her. I open my eyes. Ava wraps her arms around her dad, and I watch as he holds her and kisses the top of her head. "Are you sure you're feeling okay, sweetheart? Do you need anything? At least let me go get you some food," he says, pulling back to look at her.

"Okay, maybe just a salad or something would be good." Ava smiles up at him.

"I'll see what I can do." He nods before walking out the door. And as soon as it closes, Ava spins around and sees that I'm awake. She walks over to my bed, leans down, and kisses my lips gently.

I should tell her not to. It's wrong for me to let her kiss me. To give her the false hope that I'm going to suddenly remember her. That I'll fall in love with her again. I can't do that though. I really fucking like it when she kisses me.

"How much of that did you hear?" she asks.

"Not much. But your father's right. You shouldn't be sleeping on a chair. You really should go home tonight and sleep in your bed."

"I'm scared that if I leave, you'll disappear again."

Well, fuck. I don't think I've ever had anyone love me as much as this girl clearly does. And so openly too. It's a little overwhelming. It's also comforting in a way. I never knew I wanted that. Is it fair to take that kind of love from her when I can't give it back?

The door opens and her dad comes in with an armful of food and drinks. He stops when he realizes I'm awake.

"Ah, Dad, this is Noah. Noah, my dad." Ava puts herself between us.

"Mr Williamson, it's nice to meet you. I do wish it were under better circumstances," I say.

"What better circumstances would that be, Noah? Perhaps one where my eighteen-year-old daughter isn't left pregnant and heartbroken?" he grunts out.

"Dad, stop. You promised," Ava hisses.

"Sorry, sweetheart." He looks at his daughter lovingly. "Noah, I do hope you make a full recovery from your injuries. If there's anything you need at all, let us know."

I nod. I'm not sure what on earth he thinks I'd ever need from him. Does he realise my net worth is probably ten times what his might be?

"Ava, I'll see you for dinner. Your mum's dropping in this afternoon. Get a ride home with her." He kisses his daughter on the cheek and then leaves without looking back.

I watch as Ava lets out a long, slow breath. Her body relaxes and she smiles at me. "Well, that went better than expected."

"What were you expecting?" My eyebrows raise.

"That you'd be leaving here in a body bag, and I'd have to tell my child how Grandpa killed Daddy." She laughs.

Daddy. That word brings a smile to my lips.

28

I spent all day sitting in the hospital room with Noah. We've talked about everything and anything. I've tried to tell him stories about things we've done together, in an attempt to jog his memory. All it did was make him shut down more and more. I could see him withdrawing from me. So I stopped rehashing the past and started to talk about the future. Started to adjust the plan.

He's been in and out of sleep all day. Every time he closes his eyes, he wakes up screaming. In pain. Stuck in the nightmare of whatever happened to him over there. And it breaks my heart. I want to help him. I just don't know how. I want to take away his pain. I'd gladly bear that burden for him if I could.

We're playing cards now, and Noah is kicking my ass in *Go Fish*. Yes, we've been playing children's games. Noah says we should brush up on our skills, considering we're about to spend years playing these sorts of things with our child. I did point out that it will be a while before this baby can even read the cards, let alone learn the rules.

"Seven?" I ask him.

"Go fish." His lips tilt up at one side.

"Knock, knock." My head turns to see my mum walking through the door with a huge bouquet of sunflowers. "How's the patient?" she asks, placing the vase on the bedside table.

"Ah, okay. Thanks." Noah's eyebrows draw down in confusion.

"Good. Ava, how are you?" Mum comes over and hugs me.

"I'm fine." The response has become my go-to, no matter how I'm really feeling.

"Mmhmm." Mum doesn't say anything but I know she *knows*. "Is there anything you need, Noah? Have the doctors been in to see you today?"

"Um, yeah. I'm good. Thanks, Mrs Williamson." Noah looks to me.

"It's Alyssa. We're family, Noah, no need for formalities." Mum glances in my direction. "I didn't know what you liked to read so I got one of each." She removes a stack of magazines from a bag and places them on the table by Noah's bedside.

"You didn't have to do that..." he responds.

"It's nothing. I also smuggled in the good stuff," she says, pulling out a block of Cadbury Dairy Milk chocolate.

"Shit, that *is* the good stuff. Thanks." Noah smiles. And it's a real smile.

"You're welcome," Mum replies. "Ava, Dad said you're coming home for dinner. You ready to head out?"

"Actually, I'm just gonna stay here and..."

"She's ready. She's hardly eaten anything at all today," Noah interrupts me.

"I've eaten," I argue.

"Ava, go home and have dinner with your family. Sleep in your own bed," he says more firmly.

I don't want to leave. I want to stay here. What if I go and something happens? I should be here... What if he needs me?

"Ava, I'll be fine. I'll still be here tomorrow. It's not like I can run off." He smirks.

"Sweetheart, walk me out," Mum says. "Noah, let me know if you need anything at all." I follow Mum to the hall. She hugs me, then leans in to whisper in my ear, "Ava, I know you don't want to leave him here, but he needs time. You have to remember that you're a stranger to him. I want you to come home. Have dinner at least."

My mum is right. I don't want her to be, but she is. I need to give Noah space. *Time.* I need to be more understanding. I nod my head. I walk back over to his bedside, and without thinking, lean down and kiss him. As I'm about to pull away, he takes hold of the back of my neck, keeping my lips sealed to his for just a moment longer. I sigh into his embrace. I miss this. I miss him.

I've just spent the whole day with him, and even though he's *here*, it's not the same. He's not the same. I'm not sure if it's just because he doesn't remember me, remember us, or if it's what happened to him that's weighing him down.

"I love you. I'll be back in the morning," I promise as I straighten up. Noah smiles but doesn't say anything back.

With my heart a mix of being broken and mended, I meet my mother on the other side of the door. The whole way home, I've thought about nothing but turning around and running back to him. I don't care if he doesn't know who I am. I know who he is. And that has to be enough.

~

I'VE JUST FINISHED SHOWERING before getting dressed in a pair of yoga pants and a baggy t-shirt. I'm sitting on my bed, scrolling through my phone, when my older brother walks up.

"You know, most people knock before barging in. What if I was naked, Ash?" I ask him.

He visibly shudders. "Not an image I need in my head, Ava. Ever," he groans.

"Well, knock next time," I remind him, knowing full well he won't. I don't know if I've ever seen Ash knock on a door. He always just seems to own every room he enters. Or at least he likes to think he does.

However, this time I go easy on him because he's not alone. He has Faith in his arms. A tiny little baby I've been avoiding. I've seen the photos. I've heard my parents talk about her nonstop, but I've yet to actually meet her.

"I have someone who wants to meet her favourite aunty." Ash smiles as he sits next to me on the bed. I should have expected that he'd show up with her sooner or later. There's only so long my brother will let anyone avoid him.

Now that I'm looking down at the beautiful little baby in his arms, I regret not making the effort first. "Can I hold her?" I ask him.

"Of course, here. Support her head." He hands her over, but hovers, almost like he thinks he needs to be ready to catch her if she falls.

I stare at her perfect little face. "She's beautiful, Ash," I tell him.

"You know, she reminds me of you when you were a baby." He smiles. "How're you doing, Ava? Really doing. I don't want to hear the bullshit *I'm fine* nonsense you've been feeding everyone else."

"I'm..." I stop myself. "I don't know. Honestly, I don't know. He doesn't remember me, Ash. He doesn't remember that we were an *us*. He doesn't know that he loves me."

"Mum said his memories could come back."

"*Could...* But what if they don't? What if he doesn't fall in love with me again?" I ask the question that's been weighing on my mind.

"That's not possible. I saw the way he looked at you before he left. I saw how much he loved you. He called me when he was overseas, Ava. I heard it in his voice then too. There's no way he's not going to fall for you again." Ash wraps an arm around me.

Letting my head rest on his shoulder, I whisper, "I hope you're right."

"I'm always right, Ava," he announces, so self-assured, and I laugh.

"It's hard to believe that I'm growing one of these inside me right now." I stare at the baby in my arms.

Ash groans. "When's your doctor appointment?" he asks.

"Um, Thursday. Why?"

"I'm coming with you," he says it like it's a done deal. Like I don't get a choice in the matter.

"You don't have to do that. Mum will come with me," I tell him.

"Ava, you're having my first niece or nephew. I'm not missing any of it."

I shake my head. "Ash, uncles are not meant to be at appointments."

"Well, I'm not just any uncle. I'm going to be the best one this kid of yours has."

"I heard that," Axe calls out, walking into the room.

"You hearing it doesn't make it any less true, Axe," Ash replies.

"Ava, tell him I'm your favourite. Therefore, I'll automatically be the child's favourite too. That's how it works."

I look from one brother to the other. "I love you guys, so much." Tears stream down my cheeks. "I don't know how I got so lucky to draw the world's best brothers but I'm glad I did."

"It's going to be okay, Ava. We've got you. Always," Ash says.

"Always," Axe repeats.

DINNER WENT BETTER THAN EXPECTED. I got to hog all the cuddles from Faith because everyone is tiptoeing around, not wanting to upset me. I wish they wouldn't, but I'm not above using it to my advantage either.

I've since been lying in bed, tossing and turning, unable to shut my mind off. What if Noah wakes up with nightmares again and I'm not there to help him? I should be there. The guilt is eating me up.

Deciding I'm not going to get any sleep anyway, I throw the blankets back and jump out of bed. I slide on my shoes and pick up my keys. I'm driving to the hospital. I need to be there. It's like there's an invisible rope tethering me to Noah, pulling me in his direction.

However, my attempts at sneaking out of the house don't go as planned. I was hoping to go unnoticed, but my dad is sitting in the living room. He looks up as I try my best to tiptoe past the door.

"Going somewhere, Ava?" he asks, a hint of a smile on his lips.

"I'm going back to the hospital. I have to."

"Did something happen?"

"No, but I just... I need to be there, Dad." I decide to leave out the part about *needing to be with him.* My dad's taking this whole teenage pregnancy news really well so far. I'm still waiting for him to lose his mind. Maybe reality hasn't settled in.

He looks at me, silently observing my face before nodding his head. "I'll drive you. You're not driving around by yourself in the middle of the night."

"You don't have to do that. Why are you awake anyway?" I ask.

"Waiting to catch your brother when he sneaks back into the house." He laughs.

Once we arrive at the hospital, my dad parks the car and escorts me to Noah's ward. "Thank you." I wrap my arms around him. There's just something so comforting about my dad's hugs.

"Anytime. Call me if you need anything," he says.

I nod my head and make my way to Noah's room.

29

I wake up and it's the same old song and dance. My voice is hoarse from screaming and sweat is dripping down my forehead. For the first few moments after I open my eyes, I'm still there. Standing in that fucking hallway, in front of a suicide bomber. Except I can't run. I can't move. All I can do is stand and watch as the fucker releases the red button he's holding.

"Noah, it's okay. You're home. It's okay." Once again, that angelic voice breaks through my night terror.

I turn my head and see her. Ava. I don't even care if I'm still dreaming at this point, because she came back. I don't know why, but spending the day with her helped me more than I'm willing to admit. Her touch has an odd calming effect over me.

"You came back?" I ask, still unsure if it's really her.

"I will always come back to you, Noah."

She leans down, lightly pressing her lips to mine. And just like the times before I can't help but think: *I shouldn't let her kiss me. It isn't right.* I don't even know her, yet some part of me deep down is certain that I do. I just wish I could fucking remember. Her lips are soft. I groan as she pulls away. I don't want her to stop. I really fucking like kissing this girl.

"Want to talk about it?" she asks.

"Nope." My answer is short. There's no way I want to taint her with the nightmares plaguing me.

"Okay, how can I help?"

"You being here helps, but you really should be in bed. You need to take care of yourself, Ava."

"I couldn't sleep."

"Mmm, climb in. Lie down with me." I'm going to Hell for keeping her here and not sending her away. I have no doubt Ava could do so much better than someone like me. Then again, she's already pregnant with my kid, so I guess she's stuck with me anyway.

"I can't. I don't want to hurt you." She looks at the bed, then my leg.

"You can't hurt me any more than I already am, babe. Besides, you're practically pint-sized. You're hardly gonna take up any room." I laugh, and then regret it because everything fucking aches. She's silent as she bites into her bottom lip. Fuck, why does everything about this girl turn me on? "Please," I practically beg.

"Okay, but if I hurt you, just tell me and I'll get up," she says, climbing onto the bed. I grit my teeth as the movement sends a radiating pain up my leg.

She settles in the crook of my shoulder, and the moment my arm wraps around her, a familiarity hits me in the chest. A feeling kind of like déjà vu, I guess. I've done this before, held her in my arms. I know I have. I just wish I could fucking remember it.

It's only minutes before Ava's body completely relaxes and her soft snores sound beside me. She must be fucking exhausted. I hold her a little tighter.

"WHAT'S GOING ON HERE? She can't be in that bed with you, Mr Hunt." A nurse looms over the side rail.

"Try to move her and I'll have you fired. She needs to sleep." My whispered threat is harsh, the death stare I send her even harsher.

"It's hospital policy. She can't be in the bed with

you."

"I don't give a fuck about your hospital policy. I'm sure you've seen the name plastered throughout the building—*my name*. My family donates a lot of money to ensure you have a job. If I want her in the bed with me, I'll fucking have her in the bed with me," I growl.

Ava stirs. Blinking her lashes open, she looks over at me. "What's wrong?" She shifts and pushes herself upright, running her eyes along the length of me.

"Nothing. Go back to sleep."

"Miss, you can't be in the bed with him," the nurse says to Ava.

"Ignore her, Ava. She won't be working here much longer." I hold her tighter when she tries to move.

"It's fine, Noah. I need to get up anyway." Ava hops off the bed and I feel the loss immediately. I don't know why the fuck I'm so attached to her. She excuses herself and walks around the irate nurse, shutting the bathroom door behind her. I glare at the woman as she goes about writing something down in my chart.

"I'll be back in an hour to top up your pain medication, Mr Hunt." With that, the nurse walks out and someone else walks in.

Someone I could go a thousand years without seeing. My mother. "Noah, care to explain what you were thinking with this nonsense?" No *hello, son, how are you?* Nothing. She just waves a stack of papers in front of my face.

"What the fuck are you talking about?" I ask her.

The quicker I uncover the motive behind her visit, the quicker she'll go back where she came from. I really fucking hope I can get her to leave before Ava comes out of that bathroom.

"Your will, Noah, and some trust account you had set up for some girl. Are you insane? You must be, because I can't think of any other reason you'd give all of our money away to a stranger." She drops the papers on my chest.

I pick them up, read through the stack, and sure enough I left everything in the estate to Ava. I named her sole beneficiary. It also appears that I set up a ten-billion-dollar trust fund in her name. Huh, if she really does have that trust fund, then there's no reason for her to be sticking around here in hopes of getting money out of me. She already has it.

"She's not a stranger, Mother. She's the woman I plan on marrying. And it's not *our* money. It's my money. Grandad left it to me, not you," I say through gritted teeth.

"Yeah, well, he was another Hunt who was out of his mind. This won't stand, Noah. I won't let you hand our family's legacy over to some girl."

"You don't have a choice. Now, if that's all, you can leave." Just as I say that, Ava steps out of the bathroom.

My mother spins around to face her. "So, you're the girl who's got her claws stuck in my son. Enjoy it while it lasts, sweetheart, because I'll have you out on the curb before you can blink."

"That's enough. Get the fuck out now. And if you ever think about even looking in her direction again, I'll have you cut off from everything."

Ava appears shocked, rooted to the spot just outside the bathroom door. She hasn't spoken a single word.

"This isn't over, Noah. Your father and I are entitled to this money." My mother storms out of the room.

Ava sits down in the chair near my bed. "Well, she seems delightful."

"Don't worry about her. That woman's bark is far worse than her bite. She knows there's not a damn thing she can do about anything."

"What is she upset over anyway?" Ava asks.

"When my grandfather died, he left everything to me. My parents get a living allowance from the estate. It seems I named you sole beneficiary in my will, meaning they'd get nothing and you'd inherit the entire Hunt family fortune."

"You need to change that, Noah. I don't want your money." She sighs.

"I know you don't. But you're going to be the mother of my child. I'm not changing it." I know it's crazy—maybe I am a little insane leaving it all to Ava —but there's a reason I did that. I might not remember what it is, but I know without a doubt that I wouldn't have made that decision on a whim. She obviously meant a great deal to me.

30

Two months later

Noah's been home for two weeks now. I've hardly left his side since he returned. His physical injuries might be mending, but his mental ones are what have me worried. He hardly sleeps, he's moody, and I often find him just staring off into space, almost like he's not even in the same room as his body.

I don't know where he goes. He won't tell me what

happened. He still doesn't remember me, but that's okay. Because even though he hasn't said it, I know he loves me. I can feel it every time he holds me. And whenever he looks at me the way he used to look at me before he was deployed—when his mind is clear of his demons—it's almost like I've got him back. It just doesn't last long.

I don't need to reach over to the other side of the bed to know it's empty. It's always empty. I wake multiple times throughout the night to find Noah up and pacing the apartment. Or sitting on the balcony and staring out into the city. This time is no different. I slide out of bed, guide my feet into a pair of slippers, and throw on one of Noah's hoodies. I walk into the living room and find Noah sitting on the sofa. In the dark.

"Noah?" I ask, approaching him.

"Ava, go back to bed, babe."

Ignoring the request, I kneel down in front of him. "I'm not going anywhere. Noah, just let me help you. Let me help."

He shakes his head. "You can't help, babe. Nobody can." His palm cups the side of my face. "I don't know what I did to deserve you, but I'm fucking glad you're here."

"I love you. I will always love you, Noah." I lean into his touch.

"Marry me," he says.

My eyes widen. "No, you can't ask me that here.

This isn't what you wanted." I've read and reread the letters he wrote to me over and over. Whenever I feel sad or like all hope is lost, I read one of those letters to remind myself that he does love me. I don't need to hear the words from him. I have them in writing.

"What do you mean *no*? I love you, Ava. I want you to be my wife."

I've waited months to hear those three words from him. *Months.* He used to say them so often I took them for granted. And now he just says them like they aren't sending my already emotional hormones into overdrive.

Noah wipes the tears from my cheeks. "What's wrong? What did I do? We don't have to get married. I can handle living in sin with you." His lips tip up at the corners but I can see the hurt in his eyes.

"It's not that. It's just... you haven't said that since you've been back."

"Haven't said what?"

"I love you. You haven't told me that for so long. I just... I really missed hearing it."

"I love you. I might not remember loving you before, but I love you now. I can't imagine not having you in my life, Ava. I know I'm messed up. I know it's not easy living with me, but I will do whatever it takes to get back to the way I was."

"Technically, I don't live with you," I tease.

"*Technically*, just try to sleep somewhere else at night." He smiles.

I lean in and meld my lips with his, then an idea hits me. I know what I need to do. I can't say yes to him here. I need to take him somewhere else so he can ask me again.

"Go and get dressed. We're going for a drive," I tell him, jumping up and walking into the kitchen to grab my keys from the counter.

"Where are we going?" Noah follows me.

"I want to show you something. Just go and get dressed. Trust me." I shove him down the hallway towards the bedroom.

THE TWO-HOUR DRIVE to the lookout is silent, though not awkward, as we each get lost in our own thoughts. When I pull into the carpark, he looks around like he's scoping the place out. We're the only ones here. "Is this where you throw me off the cliff?" he jokes.

"Not funny, and no."

"Where are we?" he asks.

"The first night I met you properly, you brought me up here. So I thought it was time I brought you back." I sit in the car and stare out at the sky. It's not like in the city. Here, you can see all the stars. It's peaceful. I don't know why we haven't visited sooner. "Come on." I jump out of the car and meet him at the front. Taking his hand, I lead him towards the bench seat. Then I enable the torch button on my phone. Noah is still using a crutch to get around. I don't want him tripping on the uneven gravel. "Sit," I tell him, gesturing to the bench.

"You do know most people come to places like this during the day, when you can actually see the view," he says.

"I know. Just look out into the darkness. What do you see?" I ask him as I do the same.

"That's the thing... I don't see anything. It's pitch-black out there, babe."

"Just look again, please," I plead with him.

He turns his head towards the darkness and we sit there silently. Then he picks up my hand and inter-twines our fingers. He doesn't speak. He just continues to stare out. I peek across at him and notice the shiny wetness falling down his face.

"Noah? What's wrong?"

"I see it," he whispers.

"What do you see?" I ask, holding my breath.

"I see everything. I see you... dancing. I see everything, Ava. I-I remember." He pivots his body to look at me. "Oh God, I remember it all. I remember everything." The tears continue to roll across his cheeks. I'm speechless, almost like I'm too afraid to say anything. If this is a dream and I suddenly wake up, I don't know if I can handle that. "Ava, babe. I remember. I fucking see everything," he repeats.

"Oh my God, Noah!" I wrap my arms around his neck. "Thank God."

His arms squeeze me tight. "I'm so sorry, Ava. I can't believe what I've put you through."

"No, this isn't your fault. It's no one's fault. We're going to be okay. We're going to be fine."

He places his hand over the bump on my stomach. "I said some really nasty shit to you, Ava. I'm so fucking sorry. I'll never forgive myself for that."

"It's okay. Noah, ask me again."

"Ask you what?"

"What you asked me in the apartment tonight. Ask me again. *Here.* This is where you wanted to ask that question. Now ask me again."

"Ava Williamson, you're my everything. I don't want to go a single day without you by my side. Will you marry me?"

"Yes," I say right before he slams his lips onto mine.

TWO YEARS LATER

Noah

I watch as Ava dances around with our little girl, Annabel, in her arms. She's a natural. We might be young, but this is exactly the life I want to be living. Ava and Annabel are my entire world. Ava hasn't returned to ballet, but she has started dancing around the house again. She says she doesn't need dance anymore. That being a mother to Annabel is all she wants to do right now. I can see she misses it though. I know her. Which is why I bought her a studio. She can use it to teach classes, or just keep it for herself.

We've finally settled the lawsuits my parents fucking brought down on us. They didn't stand a chance, and as a result of their bullshit, I've cut their living expense account by half. I couldn't cut them off completely, because as much as I hate them, they are my parents.

"Hey, I didn't hear you come in," Ava says, passing our daughter over to me. "Daddy's home, Annabel."

"Hey, princess, have you been good for Mummy?" I smother her face in kisses and she giggles.

"She's always good," Ava replies.

"Just like her mumma." I grin. "I got you a gift."

"You really need to stop buying me gifts, Noah. We're going to run out of room to put stuff." She laughs.

I look around. We've moved out of the penthouse and bought a house five minutes away from her parents. With seven bedrooms. I hardly think we're going to run out of room anytime soon.

"It's not that kind of gift. Come on, we're going for a drive." I pick up the baby bag and head out to the car. Buckling Annabel in first, I then walk around and open the passenger side door for Ava.

"Thank you. Where are we going?" she asks.

"You'll see. It's a surprise."

"I hate surprises, Noah."

"No, you don't." I laugh. She does, but only because she's impatient.

"Argh, just give me a clue, a tiny little clue."

"Nope." I lift her hand and bring it to my lips. "Mrs Hunt, you're gonna have to be patient." I never miss an opportunity to call her that—the fact that she married me still amazes me. She's way out of my fucking league.

We got married on our lookout, with her entire family surrounding us. It was touch-and-go there for a while. I thought her father was going to throw me off the cliff. Even today, I still get the feeling he wants to bury me somewhere in a shallow grave. He's great to my girls, though, so I ignore the looming threats. Besides, I get it. If some asshole came around my daughter, I'd probably want to kill him too.

The dance studio is only ten minutes from the house. I pull into the carpark at the back and jump out. I open Ava's door and then unbuckle an excited Annabel. "Da-da-da," she squeals.

Every time she calls my name, my heart fucking melts. "Come on, princess, let's show Mumma her surprise." I take Ava's hand. "Close your eyes," I say, releasing her palm to unlock the door. "Okay, come in. No peeking yet." I guide her to the middle of the room. "Okay, you can look now."

I set Annabel on the ground and she runs straight for the wall of mirrors. She loves staring at her reflection. I don't blame her. She's the cutest fucking baby

I've ever seen. I like staring at her too. Ava spins around in a circle.

"You brought me to a dance studio?" she asks, confused.

"No, I *bought* you a dance studio."

"You... what? Why?" she stutters.

"You miss dancing. I know you say you don't, but I know you do. You can do whatever you want with this space, babe. It's yours. Teach Annabel to dance here. Teach lots of kids. Or just use it for yourself."

"This is... perfect." She jumps on me, wrapping her legs around my waist. "I love it. Thank you."

"I love you, Mrs Hunt. Now, I may have also packed your pointe shoes. Annabel and I are going to sit over there, and you're going to get reacquainted with the dance floor." For the next hour, I hold Annabel in my lap as we watch Ava float around the room.

I know I said she missed dancing. But the truth is, I fucking missed watching her dance just as much.

HAVE you seen where the Merged world began? It all started with Zac and Alyssa in Merged With Him Continue reading for a sneak peak ate how it all began.

ACKNOWLEDGMENTS

First, I'd like to acknowledge you, the reader. Without you, I would not be where I am today. Your constant support and feedback (through your messages and reviews) mean the world to me. They give me the encouragement to keep at this authoring journey. I love everything about conjuring up a story and putting it into words.

My Patrons: I've had so much fun on Patreon this month, creating bonus content, being able to share chapters, book covers, and everything early. Tawny, Shawna, Kayla, Jenna, Juliet, Megan, Ashley and Sam (my VIP Steamers on Patreon): I appreciate your continued support.

I would not be able to do this without the support of my husband. Nate is my happily ever after, my forever person. The one who supports me unconditionally like no one else ever has.

My beta readers are bloody amazing women. Natasha, Amy, Sam, Mel, and Vicki: you girls keep me on my toes, keep me reaching and meeting my deadlines. And make sure I'm not killing off the most important characters! I can't even imagine doing this without you girls.

Last but most definitely not least, my editor, Kat. She's my absolute favourite editor to work with, and I wouldn't want to do this bookish life without her. Also, it helps that I know I'm her favourite author!

ABOUT THE AUTHOR

kylie kent

SEXY, ALWAYS AND FOREVER ROMANCE

Kylie made the leap from kindergarten teacher to romance author, living out her dream to deliver sexy, always and forever romances. She loves a happily ever after story with tons of built-in steam.

She currently resides in Perth, Australia and when she is not dreaming up the latest romance, she can be found spending time with her three children and her husband of twenty years, her very own real-life instant-love.

Kylie loves to hear from her readers; you can reach her at: author.kylie.kent@gmail.com

Printed in Great Britain
by Amazon